MAKE IT burn

JESSIE HARPER

Cover Design: Y'all That Graphic

Editing: Librum Artis and Austin Ryan

Ebook ISBN: 978-1-7350961-7-9

Print Book ISBN: 978-1-7350961-9-3

❀ Created with Vellum

ALSO BY JESSIE HARPER

The Mint Springs Series

Make It Shine

The Finally Falling Series

Fight For It

Forget About It

Fix It

Hadley

"You really are a miracle worker. I thought no one'd be able to fix that bleach job, but you did it."

I try to take that compliment without delivering the sassy retort I have in my back pocket for Olivia Bailey. It's not about the bad dye job. I am a hair care professional. It goes without saying if a client comes into the salon with a hair emergency, I will move heaven and earth to have him or her leaving here looking like the cover model from a fashion magazine. What I'm having trouble keeping to myself is the tongue-lashing Olivia should be getting for even letting her cousin anywhere near her head. I've worked hard to get her color just right, and she went and threw that all away for a drunken experiment with a box of Clairol from the drugstore. I don't need to ask what possessed her to do such a reckless thing; I've seen Olivia's decision-making skills on display since we were in kindergarten. She is not the sharpest tool in the shed, and Fireball doesn't improve the situation. I take a deep breath and try to channel my inner Dolly. What would Dolly do? She'd give a little grace. I try to muster some of that up while I put the finishing touches on Olivia's hair.

"Well, there's a big difference in a professional and an amateur when it comes to cut and color. You shouldn't skimp on something you have to wear every day of your life."

And I do not mean that in an offhand way. Mint Springs, Georgia might not be New York City or even Atlanta, but my clients deserve to have the same experience they'd get in an upscale salon. Hot House Flowers might not be able to compete when it comes to ambiance and decor—the checkered valances from 1968 on our windows can attest to that—but there's not a stylist in here who's subpar. My mama makes sure of that. To rent a chair in our family salon you have to be top notch. This is a small town, but that doesn't mean we want to look like we just rolled off the turnip truck.

I unfasten the drape from around Olivia's neck and give her blonde curls a final shake. She smiles as I fluff the front a bit. I do not believe the higher the hair the closer to God, but a little volume never hurt anyone.

"And thanks again for working me in today, Hadley. I know it meant staying later than you planned. Hope I didn't ruin any plans you've got for tonight." Olivia raises an eyebrow at my reflection in the mirror and keeps her butt in the salon chair. She's waiting for me to give her all the details of a single girl's Saturday night before she heads home to her husband and house full of kids. I'm not exactly living the dream when it comes to my social calendar, but tonight at least, I have something to report.

"It was no trouble at all," I lie, because Olivia has actually made me a little late to the first date I've had in months. "I'm meeting Jennings at Bootlegger for a drink. I told him I'd be there as soon as I was done beautifying you."

"Jennings?" Olivia's bottom lip comes out and she eyes me quizzically. "Jennings Murphy?"

"Yep." Jennings Murphy—respectable local boy. Not the most handsome man in town, but steady, reliable, and interested.

"I thought you were seeing Cooper Allen?"

"Cooper Allen? Lord, no." I shake my head, letting my own blonde curls emphasize how emphatic that no really is. Cooper Allen should be so lucky.

"But you had something going on that summer after high school, right? And he's back now... I guess I just assumed." Olivia draws out the last word. She thinks there's more to this story, and she's not going to move from the swivel chair until I tell her everything. Well, there's nothing to know about me and Cooper, so Olivia's about to be disappointed. One teenage summer fling does not a happily ever after make. I go ahead and use the foot pedal to lower her so there's no excuse for her not to get moving.

"He's back, but there's nothing between us." I shrug. I won't bad-mouth Cooper in front of a customer, even if he would never find out. He would, of course, because in Mint Springs anything you say eventually comes right back around. Then he'd know for sure how badly he hurt me when he came back to town nearly two years ago and didn't seem to remember a thing about that summer—the one where I thought I'd found something so special.

"But he's so handsome! And now that his family's fixing up their farm, I thought maybe you two would, I don't know..."

"Nope. There is nothing between me and Cooper. Never will be. We were just kids and that was nearly ten years ago now, anyway." I give Olivia another smile. "I do need to get going. Don't want to keep Jennings waiting too long." I turn the chair, pointing Olivia toward what counts as the front desk.

"Of course! I'm so sorry for keeping you. Tell Jennings I said hello. Probably won't be long before you two are going to couples' night at the church. That's where I'm going now."

I die a little inside. I'm not quite ready yet to commit myself to every part of small-town married life. "We'll see," I say as I usher her over to the little wooden table by the front door. "Do you want to go ahead and make another appointment?"

Olivia shakes her head. "I'll give you a call. This should last a bit, don't you think?"

Oh, the color will last, but it won't be any match for Olivia's cousin, if she gets out the cheap bottle blonde again. I ring Olivia up and take her credit card. We've finally come out of the 1960s in our payment options, although several older ladies still like to write a check after their wash and set. My grandmother insists on keeping that available, especially since she's still wary of all things Internet. Hot House Flowers started out in her house, washing hair in the kitchen sink. She graduated to a shop through an addition my grandpa tacked onto their tiny one-bedroom house, and, eventually, to this place we have now. Her new house is out back so she can still keep an eye on everything. She's sure to notice the lights on over here in a minute or two.

"Well, good luck with Jennings. Maybe he's the one," Olivia excitedly tells me as she leaves the shop. "I'll keep my fingers crossed."

"Thanks." I close the door and turn the bolt. I appreciate Olivia's optimism, but I don't have much of it myself. It's been a long time since I've believed in the kind of love she seems to think is out there for me. But maybe there'll be a spark tonight between me and Jennings Murphy. Other people have found it, so why can't I?

I give my hair one last fluff before I turn out the salon lights. Jennings might not be my prince charming, but I'm sure as hell not going to waste an opportunity to find out, and I'm going to look my best doing it. You can be sure of that.

That's a Hadley Crawford guarantee.

2

Cooper

"You're staring."

"No, I'm not."

"Yeah, you are, and if you don't cut it out, she's going to look over here and catch you doing it."

I scowl at my brother. "What? Now I can't even look at her?"

"Not if it means the two of you fighting in the middle of Bootlegger. Leave Hadley alone. Drink your beer." Chance lifts his own beer to his lips. "I'm serious. We're not staying here if you can't stop mooning over her."

"Mooning?" My top lip raises in a snarl. "I'm wondering what she's doing here drinking by herself, that's all." And why she's pulled out all the stops. Hadley's long legs taunt me from over on her barstool. Would it kill her to wear a pair of pants once in a while? She's got her usual whiskey on the rocks in front of her, and her eyes are glued to her phone. I flinch when she looks up and makes eye contact with me, her eyes narrowing to slits.

"Now you've done it."

"I'm looking at the drink specials. Can I help it if the chalkboard's right above her head?" I give Hadley a nod that sends her bright red lips into an angry pucker.

"You plannin' on ordering an Appletini next?" Chance tries to hide his smirk behind his glass.

"At Bootlegger?" I shudder. "This place is beer and whiskey only. You know that." Which begs the question, why is Hadley Crawford sitting alone in this beast of a bar on a Saturday night?

Any other place she'd have been swarmed by now. There'd be a line around the block to buy her a drink. Hell, I'd be first in line if she didn't hate my guts. But it's better this way. Hadley does not need to waste her time with me. This does not, of course, stop me from getting up with every intention of going over to her.

"Are you crazy? Sit your ass back down." Chance kicks my chair toward me, bumping it into my legs.

"What's that saying? The friend of my friend is also my friend? Something like that? Lily's your wife, and she's my friend. Hadley is Lily's best friend. Ergo, Hadley is my friend too. I'm just going to make sure she realizes she's dressed up in a dive bar on a Saturday night."

"That saying's about *enemies*, Cooper. The *enemy* of your *enemy* is your friend. Hadley's not going to want to talk to you and using 'ergo' isn't going to change any of that." Chance blows out an exaggerated breath. "How do you manage on your own?"

"I manage fine. Now, if you'll excuse me..." I give my brother a little bow and start the walk toward the woman who hates me more than any other.

Hadley's angry face does not deter me from pulling out the stool next to hers and making myself at home. If anything, I love her mad face more than her happy one—

maybe because it's the one I see most often. It's familiar, if you will. Her cheekbones are already flushed with annoyance before I even open my mouth.

"That seat is taken," she bites out. Her hand darts out toward the stool I'm parked in.

"Looked empty to me." I motion to one of the bartenders. "You ready for another?" I turn my head to get a look at Hadley's face.

"No, thank you. I'm waiting on someone. I'll get another drink once he gets here." Her eyes narrow and her mouth sets into a pinched little line. It's easy to rile her up, and it's one of my favorite pastimes. I shouldn't get so much enjoyment out of it, but if the only other choice is Hadley ignoring me, then I'm going to choose her disdain.

"You have a date?" I inwardly wince at the strangled sound of my voice and try to ignore the stab of jealousy I feel behind my breastbone.

"Don't sound so shocked. Just because you aren't interested doesn't mean other men aren't." Hadley takes a sip of her drink.

"I'm not shocked." I try to school my features so there's not even an inkling of surprise. Of course men want to date Hadley. Any shock I'm feeling isn't because I doubt that, it's because of the sudden tightness in my chest. "Do I know him?" I reach for the glass of whiskey the bartender puts down in front of me, glad to have something to occupy my hands.

"It's Jennings Murphy, not that it's any of your business. And I'd rather you weren't sitting here when he shows up." Hadley checks her phone again. "Which should be any minute now."

"*Jennings Murphy*? The one with the overbite? Are you joking right now?" I tilt my head back and laugh. There is no way in hell Hadley's agreed to a date with Jennings Murphy, the only kid I can ever remember being too chicken to jump off the rope swing in the summer. When he was seventeen.

"He doesn't have an overbite!" Hadley turns her entire body, nearly knocking her knees into me. "And even if he did, it would be absolutely none of your concern, Cooper. None! Take your drink and go sit somewhere else."

"No wonder you're at Bootlegger! Only Jennings would think this is a great place to take a date." I give her a smug grin and take a long swig of my drink.

"For your information, I suggested meeting here. It's close to the salon." Hadley tucks a strand of hair behind her ear. "Not that I care what you think."

"Well, a warm-up drink here will certainly set the mood for romance. Y'all could play some darts." I grin again. "I cannot wait for him to get here."

"And you're the king of romance? I think we both know that's not true." Hadley rolls her eyes. "You wouldn't know how to woo a woman if your life depended on it."

Here Hadley might be right, but there's no way I can let an insult like that go. Not when she's spent time getting ready for Jennings Murphy, of all people. I can see my brother's alarmed face from across the room. He motions for me to come back to our table, nearly begs me to leave Hadley alone. And I'm going to, as soon as I get these last few words out.

I down the rest of my drink and stand. "There was a time, Hadley Crawford, when you thought I was pretty good at wooing. At least that's what you told everybody in town." I smile down at her, sure she won't have a snappy comeback for that.

And this is where I make a fatal mistake, because Hadley

never lets anyone get the last word, not if she can help it. She gasps, pulling away from me with such indignation I'm worried people will think I've slapped her. She doesn't even bother being quiet as she cusses me.

"Cooper Allen, you are a son of a bitch!" And then she throws the rest of her whiskey in my face just as Jennings Murphy walks in the door.

3

Hadley

"Damn you, Cooper Allen!" I throw my purse across the room. It lands on my couch and promptly tips over, scattering lipsticks and ball point pens across the hardwood. I stifle a scream of frustration. No need to get a noise complaint from any of the neighbors.

I take a few deep breaths and try to pull myself together. I think it's safe to say that was my first and last date with Jennings Murphy. Nothing gets things started off on the right foot like witnessing your date go all Tanya Tucker on someone. As Cooper stood there laughing, my wasted drink dripping down his ridiculously handsome face, Jennings had appeared by my side. That's what you get for showing up fifteen minutes late, buddy—way more Tanya than Dolly.

I should have insisted we leave right that minute, but I wanted to show Cooper he hadn't gotten the best of me. He had, of course, anyone could see that, but Jennings agreed to sit for a drink, bless his heart. And then he'd had to watch me glower at Cooper across the room, because of course

Cooper stayed too, nursing a beer over at a table with his brother.

"Well, that was...unexpected." Jennings' hands were actually shaking. "You have a very colorful vocabulary."

"I'm so sorry about that. I let my temper get the better of me." I had tried to seem contrite, but it was damn near impossible with Cooper staring at us.

"I had heard you and Cooper were, um, involved. I didn't realize it was so...volatile." He was drinking a light beer, and his khaki pants were pressed so meticulously that they still had an impossible crease even at the end of the day. Unless he'd gone home to change? Asking about the pants hadn't seemed like a great get-to-know-you question.

"Cooper and I aren't involved."

"It certainly looked like—"

"No matter what it *looked like*"—I tried to keep the anger out of my voice—"Cooper Allen and I are barely even acquaintances. His brother married my best friend. That is the extent of our relationship."

Jennings' face told me he'd believe that when pigs flew.

Dinner hadn't been much better. I'd learned Jennings was very actively looking for a wife, specifically one who would stay at home and raise several little Murphy children—ones who, hopefully, I couldn't help thinking, could avoid that overbite.

"But what if your wife liked working?" I asked as I poked at my overcooked salmon.

"Why would she want to do that?" Jennings had seemed genuinely perplexed. "There's plenty to do in a house with children, Hadley."

"Of course, but..." I tried to think of a polite way to say what I was thinking. "What if she needed more outside stimulation? Raising kids can be a little monotonous."

"My mother loved being at home." He shrugged and went back to his steak.

Unsurprisingly, I ended up back at home less than an hour later.

No worries. I have plenty of things I can use this Saturday night to accomplish. Jennings Murphy was not the love match everyone was waiting for. Cooper Allen had been right, not that I'd ever tell him that.

I'd let Cooper get under my skin again. *Why can't I manage to keep calm around him?* It's not a question I really care to answer. He'd spent teenage summers at his grandfather's farm and I'd fallen deeper under his spell with every new sighting of him in June. By the time August rolled around, I could usually think of nothing but Cooper. Not that he'd noticed me—until the summer he finally did. I was about to start college and he was about to finish, prepping for his last year of college football before he headed out into the world. And that summer had been magical. When he'd left, I was sure he felt the same way I did, and if fate ever put us back together, we'd pick up right where we left off. I had built him up in my head so much before he came back to town, that even if he'd been perfect, he couldn't have lived up to my expectations. I remembered someone sweet and funny, caring and smart. The Cooper here in Mint Springs now still has those qualities—or so I hear. I seldom get to see them.

None of that matters now, though. I change into some comfortable clothes, shedding the dress I'd worn in hopes of making a good impression on Jennings. I've known him long enough not to have bothered, maybe, but I'm a firm believer in taking pride in one's appearance. He'd asked me on a date, and I had dressed accordingly. He hadn't said a word about my outfit, however, and hadn't complimented me in any other way either.

I wipe the make-up from my eyes and wash off any trace of this disaster of an evening. *Cross Jennings Murphy off the list*. Luckily, I hadn't had my heart set on anything there.

I settle onto the couch with a warm blanket, my laptop, and a glass of water. I didn't drink too much tonight, but there's no need to tie one on here by myself at home. And I need to be sharp for what I'm about to do. I open the laptop and log into my account. There it is, ready and waiting for me to get started.

The last class I need to take to earn my undergraduate degree.

Entrepreneurial Marketing might not sound exciting to some people, but those people probably haven't been taking online classes for ten years, chipping away little by little at a degree. I have, and this class is all that stands between me and a diploma.

I take a look at the syllabus. I've been told this class is a beast, with a final project that makes grown men cry. I'm not intimidated by that. I've proven I can handle academic challenges; it's the other ones life throws at me that I need help mastering. If life were a bit more equitable in handing out obstacles, I think plenty of people would be sitting a little differently right about now. Me? I'd have the Ivy League diploma I'd always dreamed of, my own flourishing business, and be starting a family with a fantastic man—one who would never make me so frustrated I'd throw a drink in his face. But all of those wishes didn't come true. Well, the Ivy League part almost did. I worked my butt off in high school, Most Likely to Succeed and all that. The acceptance to Harvard had been unexpected, but deserved. The bill, however, had come as a shock.

I'd gotten over not having the money for the debutante ball. I'd been fine with secondhand clothes and none of the fancy vacations some kids had. Sure, the barbs and snide comments hurt, but I wasn't going to be here forever. I was leaving all those smart-mouthed assholes in the dust. I'd never been farther than Atlanta, but I kept thinking the universe wouldn't take Harvard away from me. It wouldn't be that cruel, would it?

That was my first real lesson in making my own way. Those loans would have been the kind I could never pay off. Then I'd overheard my grandmother talking to my mama about selling the salon to come up with my college money, renting chairs at a place they had owned just to make ends meet while I went to Boston to live my dream. I couldn't let that happen, couldn't let my family give up their dreams so I could selfishly have mine.

I told everyone I'd changed my mind.

I went to cosmetology school, became the best damn stylist I could. I'd always been good at hair and make-up and, of course, I was a quick study. I pretended college wasn't for me, all the while secretly taking classes whenever I could. The local community college had plenty of courses to get me started, and State has an online option that lets me do the work at night. I'm getting this degree come hell or high water, and I'm doing it for myself. Everyone around here might think I'm just another girl who didn't reach her potential, but I know who I am.

I add the class assignments and due dates to my planner, making sure I have plenty of time to get things done. I don't like to procrastinate, and my work schedule means I need to be organized. If this final project is as bad as I've been told, I'll want to get started as soon as possible. That's when I see the thing I hate the most.

We've been partnered up for the final project.

I groan. A partnered project for an online class? Could there be any worse torture?

A look farther down the screen tells me there can be.

My partner's the one name I recognize from the entire class roster.

Cooper Allen.

4

_____

Cooper

"Aw, hell no!" I stare at the computer screen, rub my eyes to make sure I'm not seeing things.

"What are you cussing about?" My brother comes into the kitchen, shirtless and in his boxer shorts. He grabs two mugs from the cabinet and fills them both with coffee.

"Don't drink all of that. I'm going to need at least two cups to wake up this morning." I cut him a look and go back to staring at the screen. "And could you put on some pants? Nobody needs to see that much of you this early in the morning."

"My wife would disagree." Chance smirks as he adds cream and sugar to the cup of coffee I'm sure he's bringing to Lily in bed. "And if you don't want to see any of this, you should work on getting your own house built a little faster. You are sitting in my kitchen, after all." He stirs sugar into his own cup and takes a sip. "What are you doing up this early on a Sunday, anyway?"

"I was trying to get a head start on this class I'm taking." I frown. "But I think I'm going to have to drop it."

"Drop it?" Now Chance is fully awake. "Why? Isn't it the last one you need to take? And it's the only one you were looking forward to."

"Yeah, but there's a complication." I groan and close my eyes. Chance is going to get way too much enjoyment from what I'm about to tell him. "There's a big project at the end."

"So?" He refills my coffee cup. "You're usually good with projects."

"It's a partnered project."

"Ah." Chance sits, and I have the unfortunate view of his naked chest as he rubs the stubble on his chin. "Could still be fine."

My brother knows it won't be fine. Working with someone else is never easy for me.

"It won't be. I should drop the class and look for something else. Or wait until it's offered again."

"You should give it a try. You're so close to finishing, Coop. You can't just quit."

Just quit. That's what everyone thinks I do when things get tough, when they aren't amusing anymore. Good ol' Cooper—tons of fun but lazy. The king of doesn't-give-a-shit.

"I know, but group projects aren't my thing and the person I'm supposed to work with..." I wince. I should have taken care of this without saying anything to my brother, but he caught me in an under-caffeinated moment.

"It's somebody you know?" Chance drinks more of his coffee, swirling it around in his cup. "That might be good. Easier." He's trying to be encouraging. It still burns a little to be getting a pep talk from my younger brother, sitting at the kitchen table in *his* house on the family farm he now owns free and clear. Chance has more than lapped me in the life department.

"Lily's coffee's getting cold." I nod toward her abandoned cup.

"Or is it someone immune to your good ol' boy charm?" Chance's eyes light up. "Please tell me it's one of the bartenders from Bootlegger. The new girl from the diner? You struck out pretty hard with her."

"She's not representative of my usual success rate and you know it." I scowl.

"So, who is it, then? Chance takes another gulp of his coffee.

"Hadley."

The coffee shoots from Chance's mouth all over the table.

"Watch the laptop! Jesus, Chance." I run to grab a dish towel.

"Hadley? Hadley Crawford? Hadley from the hayloft?" Chance asks.

"Yes, Hadley Crawford. And please don't bring up the hayloft. I'm already in trouble here. If Lily hears you talking about that again..." I shake my head. Hadley gave Chance that ammunition herself. I would never have told anyone about the hayloft. That had been our special spot, the place we snuck off to when we wanted to be alone. I've got plenty of memories of Hadley and I tangled together skin to skin, hoping no one else would come looking for us in the barn. I shake those images away. I'm not even supposed to remember any of that, anyway. That's what I pretended when I saw her for the first time when I came back to town, when I set things in motion so she'd be sure to steer clear.

Maybe I would have handled it better if I'd had some warning, but when Hadley had shown up unannounced at the barn with Lily, I panicked. Chance had moved to Mint Springs temporarily to fix up the farmhouse. We all assumed it'd end up for sale, but Chance opted to buy it and make this his permanent home. Before all that had been decided, though, I'd started coming up every weekend to lend a hand, to try to be the helpful big brother I don't often get the opportunity to be. That first Saturday we were repairing the barn when an unfamiliar car had rolled up the gravel drive.

Hadley.

I thought she'd be long gone—would have left Mint Springs for some fancy life. She had big plans that summer we were together, and I'd never doubted she was going to get everything she wanted and then some. Instead, she'd been a few hours away from me the whole time, living a life I know she never wanted. Once she was standing right in front of me—short shorts and high heels I knew were meant for me, holding a blueberry pie fresh from the bakery—I didn't know what to do. She'd showed up with Lily to surprise me, and it had definitely worked. She had been here pining away the same way I had been for her, but there was no way we could pick up where we left off. Hadley was too smart and too funny to end up here—and way too smart and funny for the likes of me. I'd been too shocked to formulate any kind of a plan. When your perfect woman materializes in front of you, looking so hopeful and excited to see you that your heart breaks in two on the spot, there's only one thing to do.

Pretend you don't remember her.

Yeah, it was a terrible plan, made worse by Hadley's persistence. She couldn't believe I didn't remember her and thought maybe a few reminders would jog my memory. Her face had fallen again and again when I'd feigned ignorance. She'd given me everything that summer, and I acted like she never crossed my mind.

Then she got angry. I remember her temper, for sure, but in reality, I remember everything. You don't forget Hadley Crawford, no matter how many years have passed. But I'd hoped she'd forgotten me. Because I'm no match for Hadley, and working with her on this project is going to prove that to her.

"Lily never said anything about Hadley going back to school." Chance gives his stubble another scratch.

"Don't look at me. I have no idea what Hadley does." *As much as I might like to.* "But she's in this class, and she's partnered with me."

"You can't postpone graduating because you don't want to work with Hadley." Chance is right, of course, and any sane person would think the same thing. But when it comes to Hadley, I am not rational; last night more than proves me right. Since she never forgot me, I've made it my business to convince her to hate me. If the whiskey on my face yesterday at Bootlegger is any indication, I'm succeeding. If I were a real dick, I'd use this project to set Hadley's feelings in stone once and for all. But even I'm not that big of a jerk. I can't ruin her grade.

I open my email, already composing a note to the professor in my head. Something adequately pleading that might get me out of this situation. At the very least I can try to switch partners. But I don't get a chance to do any of that. Hadley's beat me to it.

I don't know what you think you're doing, but there's no way I'm letting you mess this up for me, Cooper. I asked the professor to partner me with someone else, but Dr. Fletcher says the pairings aren't open for discussion. Let me warn you, none of that football quarterback please-do-my-homework-for-me will work for this project. You had better pull your weight.

I'm serious.

Hadley

I can picture her determined face as I read the note, imagine the way she probably pulled her bottom lip between her teeth as she wrote it, feel my heart lurch in my chest at the thought of letting her down.

This is a disaster in the making, and now I'm all about making it.

5

Hadley

"You don't think he did that on purpose, do you?"

"Signing up for a college class so he could drive you insane? No, Hadley, I don't. How would he even have known you were taking classes? Even I didn't know." It's hard to miss the hurt in Lily's voice.

I look around the salon to make sure no one's listening. This is prime eavesdropping material right here and Hot House Flowers isn't the place to tell your secrets if you want them to stay, well, secret.

"I would have told you, it's just...it's something I've been doing for myself. And it's taken so long, I'm almost embarrassed to tell anyone. I've been working on this for years." I meet Lily's eyes in the mirror as I finish her haircut. She's come a long way from the constant ponytail she used to wear when she came back to Mint Springs. She's had some tough things in her life, and she shared them all with me. I'm sure it doesn't feel great to learn I've been keeping something from her.

"But I think it's great you've been working on your

degree; I don't understand why you wouldn't want to cele-brate that."

"I'll celebrate once I finish the damn thing. *If* I finish it, now that Cooper's mixed up in it." I sigh. I spend plenty of my time actively trying to exorcise Cooper from my thoughts. Now he's front and center, inserted in my life again in a way I can't control.

"Of course you'll finish, Hadley." Lily shakes her still wet head. "And Cooper isn't trying to keep you from that. He's trying to finish a degree, too. He needs to pass this class the same as you."

"But I don't understand why he's doing online classes at State in the first place. Wasn't he some big football star somewhere?" I know he was, because that summer, when I thought Cooper Allen was the answer to all my teenage dreams, he'd been back in town on summer break—a break cut short by his need to return to campus for preseason. He'd been a pampered athlete his entire life, with looks, charm, and the body to match. I'm sure he had money to pay for his education. There's no reason for him to be slum-ming it with me now.

"I think he washed out." Lily's brown eyes flick to mine. "He's never been particularly great with academics, I don't think. He'd kill me for telling you that. Football kept him at school, but he barely had the grades to play most of the time, from what I hear. I don't think he had enough credits to ever graduate. He's not exactly a scholar."

"That's because he gets by on his other attributes." I frown. "And now he's partnered with me for a project that's more than fifty percent of our grade. That's wonderful." I put down the scissors and reach for the blow dryer.

"He tries his best, I think." Lily doesn't look completely convinced. "Not everyone can be as smart as you, Hadley."

A lot of good it's done me. The class valedictorian, paying her tuition with tip money.

The hum of the blow dryer drowns out anything else she might say. She wouldn't be able to make me any less apprehensive, anyway. Cooper doesn't need to do well the way I do. He's got nothing to prove. He's probably used to coasting by. Well, I've warned him. He'd better be ready to work.

"Be nice." Lily mouths at me in the mirror.

I give her my sweetest smile. Me? Not nice? Never.

"Let's get one thing straight. I intend to get an A on this project. *An A*. I won't accept anything less, and I won't let you stand in my way of achieving that."

Cooper looks up from his phone and stands. "Well, hello to you too, Hadley. Glad you could join me." He gives me one of his lazy smiles, and my blood boils.

"Let's make this quick. I don't need to waste all day." I scan Patty Cakes, looking to see which notorious gossips are witnessing this meeting. Patty makes the best pastries in town, so of course, it's packed in here. Plenty of people available to spread the word that Cooper and I met for coffee at the bakery.

"Can I get you something to drink?" he asks with so much sweetness in his voice you'd swear he was one of Patty's cookies.

"No, thank you. I can get my own drink." I give Cooper a glare and stomp off to the register. I'm not wasting any smiles on the likes of him.

"You here with Cooper?" Patty asks, not making eye contact as she rings up my latte with a shake of cinnamon and blueberry muffin. She tries to act uninterested, but this isn't small talk. Patty's going to be telling this all over town, probably before I can even sit down.

"Technically, yes, I'm here with Cooper. But if you're asking if I'm *with* Cooper, the answer is no." I hand Patty a ten-dollar bill.

"I wasn't asking anything in particular." Patty hands me my change. "He sure is cute, though. Wouldn't be the worst thing in the world to have to look at that all day."

I cut my eyes to where Cooper's stretched out like a cat. His long legs stick out from under the table and protrude into the aisle. He's got his hands behind his head now, fingers laced behind his dark blond hair. He catches me looking and winks one of those hazel eyes I used to dream about.

"I can think of other things I'd much rather look at," I inform Patty, trying to remember not to take out all my Cooper-fueled frustration on an innocent bystander. "This all looks delicious." There's no reason not to be polite. "Thank you." I take my coffee and the still-warm pastry and walk back to put the fear of God in Cooper.

He stands again when I approach the table, reaching to pull out my chair. His sudden attack of chivalry has me eying him warily. I settle in my chair and take a sip of my coffee, regarding him over the rim.

"I think we've gotten off on the wrong foot." Cooper gives me the kind of smile that used to make me melt. I'm immune to that now. Cooper may be handsome, but he is also the kind of man to forget you once you're not standing in front of him. Out of sight, out of mind for Cooper and most women, I assume. Unless I'm the only one he conveniently forgot once he'd gotten what he wanted.

"Oh, when was that? That summer when I made the mistake of letting you get into my pants? Or later when you came back to town with no memory of it?" I take a bite of my muffin and take a moment to enjoy Cooper's stricken face. Delicious.

"Or maybe it was one of any number of times since then. Like, maybe the night you convinced Tanner Mathis I was a lesbian? Or the time at the Fourth of July parade when you tried to get me arrested? It was a nice touch that the officer you brought over was the one I was dating. Or perhaps the other night at Bootlegger, when I had to waste a perfectly good drink? Was that the time you're thinking of?" I take another bite and chew. I'm not yelling by any means, but I'm sure the spies at Patty's heard every word.

Cooper chokes a little on the sip of coffee he's tried to take. He shouldn't be surprised by my inability to keep my mouth shut. There was a time when he said he liked the fact I was "outspoken." It's not like I've changed much, and every time he and I cross paths—which is frequently now that Lily's married to his brother—I'm sure to raise hell about whatever he's done to me.

"First of all, I did not 'get in your pants,'" Cooper hisses at me. "You make it sound so..."

"Forgettable?"

"Jesus, Hadley." He runs his hand over his face, giving the stubble on his chin a few extra swipes. "I'm trying to explain here."

"I don't think there's anything to explain, Cooper. I thought you were someone else when I was young and naive, I guess. You've shown me the error of my ways."

Cooper's face falls. "Just so you know, I tried to convince the professor to switch partners. He didn't listen to me either. And I looked into dropping the class but it isn't offered again until next spring. I'd have to wait another year, and that would mean postponing graduation. There's nothing I can take in its place, either. I looked. I've done everything I can to keep us from working together, but it looks like we're stuck."

I pause mid-sip. "Why would you drop the class?"

"Because I'm worried about the alternative."

"You'd rather drop the class and postpone your graduation than have to work with me." My jaw hangs open a bit.

"No, Hadley—no. I'd rather drop the class than get you all jammed up. I don't want to postpone graduation, but what's another semester, give or take? A year, though? Even I can't justify that." Cooper slumps in his chair, defeated.

"Why haven't you finished already?" I've been dying to ask, so I go ahead and spit it out.

"Why haven't *you*? I thought you were on your way to Harvard, going to get that Ivy League education and take the world by storm." A smile plays on his lips, but for once I don't think he's teasing.

"Plans change, Cooper. I decided to stay here." I sit up straight. There's no shame in the choice I made, even if I don't think Cooper will understand or appreciate it. What has he ever had to give up?

"That's not what I would have thought you'd do. Not in a million years. Not after the way you talked about it. You were so excited about Boston, Hadley, I can't believe it was a change of heart. A whim." Cooper's voice has gone soft, his eyes focused on mine.

"Thought you didn't remember things like that." I try to hide my surprise behind the anger I've been stoking. That fire burns pretty bright, but it's no match for the gooey way my heart still sometimes feels when I think of Cooper and that summer. I had talked a lot about college—about my dreams for those years and what could come after. I was full of big plans.

Big plans that would never, ever come to fruition.

But finally becoming a college graduate isn't going to be like that. This is one of my plans that's going to work out.

"I remember some things," he admits, and that soft spot gets a fraction bigger.

I need to put a stop to this before I get sucked in. I'm sure that's what Cooper wants—for me to lose myself in some warm and fuzzy feeling. Then I'll do all the work and he'll coast to an easy A.

"You didn't tell me why you're still working on your undergrad. I would have thought you'd finished years ago. And at State?" I let the disdain I'm sure he feels drip from my voice. "You can't be happy to have that on your resume." I'd pictured Cooper with a corporate job and a beautiful wife, a few gorgeous children rounding out the picture, not sitting in the dark late at night grinding out assignments the same as me.

"Honestly, I'll be happy just to have something to put on my resume at all. You think I like being a thirty-two-year-old still picking along in these undergrad classes? I swear this isn't some trick, Hadley. I'm in this the same as you."

I don't want to feel anything close to sympathy for Cooper—don't want to feel anything for him at all—but I know the crushing defeat that is having your life seem smaller than you'd like, and I can see a glimmer of that in him now. Fine, we have to work together, but I don't have to like it.

"We should talk about the project." I'm all business. No feelings here, certainly not one that borders on affection for Cooper Allen.

"Fine with me."

I wait for him to shift his body, reach for a laptop or a notebook. Hell, I'd be happy with a crayon and some construction paper. But Cooper stays sitting in the wooden chair, looking at me like he needs directions.

I let out an exasperated sigh. "Well?"

"Right now?" he asks, reaching over to steal a bite of my blueberry muffin.

And just like that, any goodwill toward Cooper disappears.

6

Cooper

"Eddie Mack, where you at?"

Metal clanks from somewhere deeper in the warehouse. "Cooper? That you? Come back here and help me."

I walk through the part of the warehouse that technically counts as the "store." It's hardly a great place to try to sell anything, but no matter how many times I tell Eddie, nothing changes. He's got things stacked along the walls haphazardly, and the counter's cluttered with not only a month's worth of mail but what looks like engine parts. He claims the moonshine's the reason people come in, not the ambiance. He's right about that, because you'd have to really love moonshine to put up with this mess.

"Where are you?" I shout again, scanning the back of the cavernous warehouse. I make my way through the giant tanks and various buckets, past the giant copper still Eddie uses to make his signature moonshine.

"I'm back here. Watch your step."

Eddie's gray head's bent over some collection of metal and plastic parts, running his fingers along the edges of each piece as he pulls them from a giant box. "Got somethin' in the mail today."

"I can see that. What's it supposed to be?"

"Supposed to be parts from a mash tun, but I think I'm missing a few things." Eddie straightens up and rubs his lower back. He's wearing his usual uniform of denim overalls, and he slides his baseball cap back on his head. "I'm trying to put something together on my own. Save a little money."

"I thought you were using the open tanks for the mash?" I'm always full of questions for Eddie. He was an old friend of my grandfather's, and he makes the best moonshine in town. He was the one who originally taught me how to make small batches. It's technically illegal, and after Eddie found true love with Constance Fuller, my moonshine education came to an abrupt end. Constance could just as easily have been named Temperance, because she believed Jesus wouldn't look too kindly on making moonshine, no matter how small the batch. Eddie tried hard to save all our souls, but Constance eventually found other reasons to cut Eddie loose. He came right back to the still, and I stepped right back to my spot next to him. Luckily, he didn't seem to mind a teenage apprentice for a few months every summer.

Eddie's setup now is as legal as it gets, even if it doesn't look particularly professional. Around here you used to need a prescription for the purchase of spirits, or to pay for a tour of the distillery to get a "free" bottle thrown in as a thank you. If you had been expecting one of those professional tours at Eddie's with shiny stills and a fancy tasting at the end, you would have been disappointed. The front of the store is a disaster, with its hodgepodge of chairs and barrels Eddie keeps telling me he's going to make into tables, but the back of the house is even worse. Sure, there are health department requirements, but Eddie makes moonshine by feel. He needs to smell the mash and see how far along the fermentation's gotten to know when to move on to the next steps. Explaining this to a busload of people expecting to get tipsy on the house product isn't Eddie's forte. He makes great moonshine, but don't ask him to tell *you* how to do that in thirty minutes or less.

"I'm thinking about my set up for the sunflower liquor— what I need to control for with those seeds to be able to make the mash." Eddie's gnarled hands move over the assortment of pipes again. "Might try something more commercial."

"More commercial? Well, I never." I fold my arms across my chest and wait.

Eddie's head snaps up. "You, of all people, should be thanking me. Maybe this'll be something you can use once you get your own place set up." His dark eyes flash with irritation.

"I'm only joking, Eddie." I make sure to get my apology out there first thing. Getting on Eddie's bad side isn't ever a good idea, and I don't want him to kick me out because he didn't like my sarcasm. "I appreciate you helping me weed through all the options."

"You talk to your brother yet?" Eddie extends some of the clear tubing to me. "Hold this."

I stand there like an idiot, holding the floppy plastic tubes as I confess something Eddie's going to rake me over the coals for. "Not yet."

"Not yet?" Eddie shakes his head. "Boy, we talked about this. If you're going to set up any kind of a distillery, you need to get moving. It'll take months to get the equipment, and you'll need to be working on the space. You can't keep putting that conversation off."

"I know," I hedge. "It's just a lot of money." And it requires a level of confidence I don't quite have.

"Aren't your brothers already talking about a restaurant or something? Why haven't you put your idea out there? It's not like they don't fit together." He pulls another shiny pipe from the box, yanking off the paper it's wrapped in.

My brothers are talking about what we want to do with the farm. Now that Chance owns it, we want to make sure we can keep it. He's got plenty of money—the ridiculous amount he got paid when he sold his share of his tech business made my head spin—and he's being incredibly generous already. Charlie and Cade proposed an events space with catering. Chance and Lily had their wedding on the farm and based on the *oohs* and *ahhhs* that got, I'm sure more than a few people would pay to have their wedding there. Lily's great with design, and she and Chance are booked solid for their renovation business. After fixing up the farmhouse, they've expanded into doing that work for other people. It would make sense to have a space where we showcase all of that. But even when we've all been hunkered down around the kitchen table talking about possibilities, I've never had the courage to tell them about my idea. Yes, a whiskey distillery would fit in perfectly, but asking my brother to put more of his own money into something I can't guarantee would be a success has a stranglehold on my tongue.

"You'll need to get the permits and such as well, Cooper. It's not a small undertaking. You know that." Eddie dips his head back into the box and swings his arm around through the rest of the packing material. "There'd better be a few things left in the bottom of this here, or I'm gonna have to give them a one-star review. You can help me with that, right?"

"Leaving a review? Yes, sir, I can." That's one thing I can do, but when it comes to all the things I'll need to figure out with the legal parts of starting and running a business like this? I'm terrified of showing my ignorance there. "Let me dig around in there; my arms are longer."

I put the tubing on the floor and switch places with Eddie. I'm more comfortable keeping my hands busy than standing around watching him work.

"You've got a lot to figure out, Cooper, and I know it can seem like a challenge, but you can do this. If it's what you want, you need to talk to your brothers about it. Now's the time to get the ball rolling." Eddie knows how much it would mean to me to have something of my own, and I'm hoping this distillery idea's one the rest of my siblings will think is worth a look.

I keep my face hidden in the box, hoping Eddie won't see the fear I'm sure is plainly visible. At thirty-two, I thought I'd have something more to show for myself. This distillery might be my last shot. I need to make sure my pitch is perfect.

And suddenly I know exactly how to make sure that happens.

I run my hands around the edge of the box one more time and look up at Eddie with a smile on my face. "I think I've got something here."

Eddie grins back at me. "Let's hope so."

7

Hadley

"Mama? Mama!"

No answer.

Why is it whenever I need something in this salon, it is never where it should be? I've tried to make systems, charts, schedules—none of it works. And it's never the girls renting chairs who leave supplies out or forget to put empty bottles on the reorder list. Oh, no, it's my mother and grandmother constantly leaving me in the lurch.

I open the last set of cabinet doors in the closet we use as a store room. "Thank God!"

"What are you hollerin' about in here? We can hear you clear over at your grandma's house." My mother finally pokes her head in. "That kind of yelling disturbs the customers."

"Not nearly as much as it disturbs them to have to stop in the middle of a perm because no one refilled the neutralizer. I imagine Miss Birdie would have something colorful to say about that." I gesture to the tiny elderly woman currently sitting in my salon chair. Birdie Lee does not like to sit longer than necessary. Already she's fidgeting, hating the idle time it takes to get her hair done. I've suggested that perhaps she'd like to try a style that requires less time in the chair, but she wants the tight helmet of curls she's been wearing since 1975.

"I imagine she would." My mother tilts her own frosted head toward the open cabinet. "What was it doing in there?"

"I can give you one guess." I grab the bottle and shut the cabinet doors.

"Oh," my mother gives her head a dismissive shake. "Don't be so hard on your grandma."

"It makes it hard to work here when she moves things around. She isn't even technically a stylist anymore," I gripe, sounding more and more like a whiny teenager by the minute.

"Well, she's technically still the owner, Hadley, so I wouldn't try to start a fight with her just because you've got your panties in a wad. You've been a pill all week. What's got you all worked up?"

There's no way I can tell my mother what—or really, who—has been bothering me. And the realization that I've been stomping around Hot House Flowers like a moody adolescent has me covered in shame.

"I'm sorry, Mama. I think I'm a little tired, maybe. I should get back to Miss Birdie."

"Don't you worry about her. I think she's actually gone on ahead and fallen asleep over there."

I lean out of the closet a bit and can see Birdie Lee's eyes are closed, her roller-clad head listing a bit to the side. "I should still check on her," I whisper. She might not just be dozing. If Birdie Lee were to go to meet her maker with a head full of foam curlers here in the salon, we'd never hear the end of it.

"Let her have a nap for two seconds, Hadley." My mother steers me deeper into the closet. "Is this about a man? I heard you were out with Jennings the other night. Trouble already?"

Oh, there's trouble alright, the main trouble being Jennings' longing for a 1950s housewife. The second being that if my mama's heard about Jennings then she's heard about my fight with Cooper beforehand. "Jennings isn't a good fit."

"I think we all know why that is, Hadley. You can't exactly expect there to be sparks with anyone while you're still carrying that big ol' torch around." She gives me a little *tsk tsk*. "You've got to quit letting Cooper Allen take up so much of your energy."

"I'm not—"

"You were at Patty Cakes with him only a few days later. How is he supposed to learn if you keep forgiving him the way you do?"

"What? I haven't forgiven Cooper." My mouth falls open in surprise.

"That's sure not how it looks. You two keep dancing around each other. The rest of us are already dizzy from all this spinning." My mother folds her arms across her chest, letting her manicured nails rest on her biceps. "That's no way to catch a man. Let me give you a little advice."

"Oh, no, Mama. I really need to get back to Birdie." And the last thing I need is advice about men from my mother. Abilene Crawford is not a woman who should ever be giving advice of any kind, but especially not when it comes to men. Her track record speaks for itself. My mother has never been able to successfully manage a relationship, despite years and years of trying. She's been married four times now, although she claims one of those doesn't count since she married my father twice. And after that last divorce and his subsequent escape to Florida twenty years ago, we haven't heard from him at all. In my opinion, that should count more than double.

"I think Cooper needs to be given a little more of your sweet and less of your salty."

"Good Lord, Mama." I roll my eyes. She can make anything sound dirty without even trying. It used to make me wish the ground would swallow me up, but now I appreciate it for the super power it is.

"Hear me out. You catch more flies with honey, everyone knows that." Again, she nods like she's told me something profound.

"I don't want to attract flies. Cooper and I aren't doing some sort of courting dance; we genuinely don't like each other." I motion with the bottle of neutralizer. "I need to wake Birdie and get to rinsing."

The back door opens, and the unmistakable sound of my grandmother's shoes on the linoleum echo through the salon. Mimi's eighty-four years old and refuses to wear anything with less than a two-inch heel. Crawford women are nothing if not stubborn. It's easy to see where I get it. I'm hoping I've also inherited the same ageless skin and high metabolism. Both my grandmother and my mother look twenty years younger than they should.

"What are y'all doing in here?" my grandmother asks as she peeks her head into the supply closet. "And why's Birdie Lee out here snoring?"

"I'm giving Hadley some relationship advice." My mother motions for my grandmother to join us in the closet. "She's not being particularly receptive."

Mimi scowls. "Listen to your mama, Hadley. She has a wealth of experience when it comes to matters of the heart."

There is not enough room in this closet for the amount of Dolly Parton I'm going to need to summon to get through this. "Thank you both for your concern, but I've got Cooper Allen handled."

"The hell you do," Mimi laughs, her cackle bouncing off the walls of this too-tiny space. Once she recovers she puts on a serious face. "I thought you and Jennings would have been a nice match."

My mother also gives this a solemn nod.

I groan. "You can both stop pretending. We all know that was never going to work."

"Thank goodness! I was worried about that overbite." My grandmother lets out a relieved sigh. "I think that kind of thing's genetic, and we've spent too many generations getting this pretty to let bad teeth ruin us now."

"That's true," my mother agrees. "The Allens all have very nice teeth. Good bone structure too. And tall! Those would be some beautiful babies." She and my grandmother *cluck cluck* about the possibility.

"I am not having babies with any of the Allens!"

"Well, not Chance, since Lily made off with that one, but you were never interested in him, anyway. Cooper's a good choice, and the two of you can't seem to keep away from each other. Why are we in here again?" My grandmother looks around the closet. "How long has Birdie been out there? Past time for her rinse, I'd think."

"Shit, shit, shit!" I bolt from the closet and reach Birdie right as my timer goes off. She wakes with a start, blinking at me in the mirror.

"Let's get you over to the sink, Miss Birdie." I get her up

out of the chair and steer her by the elbow as the rest of my family escapes from the storage closet.

"Hadley here will make sure you look lovely today, Birdie," my grandmother calls as she goes out the back door. "Nothing less than perfection here at Hot House Flowers."

8

Cooper

"Did you even bother to read any of the articles I sent you?" Hadley's exasperated question assaults me.

"I looked at them. I can't be expected to read two hundred pages." I can barely keep up with the reading for class. As is, I'm up all night trying to understand what the professor's given us.

"Did you *skim*, Cooper? Can you tell me anything about the articles? Anything at all?" Hadley sighs dramatically. "We have to work on this project together. I can't do all the work. I won't." She folds her arms across her chest and glares at me.

I try to look contrite, but Hadley's arms push her already ample chest even higher. Her breasts are threatening to escape from the V-neck of her T-shirt, and that's difficult for me to ignore. I try, really try, to keep my eyes on her face, but focusing on her full lips and big blue eyes isn't helping.

There's plenty in here to distract me, in addition to Hadley. We decided to meet at her apartment to get started on our project, and now I'm looking around to see what I can figure out about the girl in front of me. I know plenty, most of it specific to teenage Hadley. A good deal of it of the carnal variety. But I've only been in her apartment once before, and that was a Lily emergency. I didn't have the opportunity to look at my leisure.

The living room's clean, not a thing out of place, and Hadley's got art on the walls and throw pillows on the couch. I don't know why I'd expected bubblegum pink walls and posters of some teen heartthrobs; obviously Hadley's a grown woman. She's got a job and a life that went on without me, just like I intended. I never pictured it like this, though—an apartment in Mint Springs and online classes to finish a degree she should have had in hand years ago. I've always known Hadley was smart, it's one of the reasons I knew I had to let her go, but working with her now, I'm reminded again of all the opportunities she should have had but for some reason gave up.

"Earth to Cooper."

"I'm listening," I lie.

"Do you have the assignment pulled up on your laptop?" Hadley's chastising me like a child. "We should look at the requirements and start to divide things up."

I pull up the lengthy description on my computer.

"What does the first part say? I'll take notes so we don't leave anything out." She pulls out a legal pad and a freshly sharpened pencil and waits for me to start reading.

I look at the words on the computer screen. I've read the assignment information before—several times, actually— but reading it out loud's another matter entirely. I've never been able to read in front of the class without stumbling, never in any way that made a teacher tell me I was doing a good job. My palms start to sweat at the possibility of Hadley hearing me struggle through even the first few sentences.

"Haven't *you* read it?" I stall.

"Of course."

"Then why do we need to read it out loud? I'm not wasting time on some kind of dinner theater, Hadley. If you want to take notes, you should take them on your own time." I sit back in my chair and stretch out my legs, cross my ankles, and try to look confident.

"I'm not asking you for a *performance*, Cooper. We need to make sure we both agree on the requirements so there aren't any surprises." Hadley's expression is stern. She means business, and I'm going to have a time getting her to give up.

"Why don't you read it to me, then?"

"Because I'm taking notes." Hadley grips the pencil tighter. "You know what, never mind."

Finally. Crisis averted.

"We need to come up with an imaginary business. Let's start there. I was thinking we could do something with a salon, since I know enough about the business side of that to keep us from doing extra research. What do you think of that idea?"

I pretend to consider what Hadley said, but in truth I've already got an idea of my own. "That could work, I guess, but I've got something else to suggest." I've thought long and hard about how to convince Hadley. If I can't get her on board, there's no way I'll be able to convince my brothers to do this for real. "How about a distillery?"

Hadley's nose wrinkles. "No."

"Now, hear me out." I sit up straight and lean forward,

trying to get Hadley's full attention. "We both like whiskey, right?"

"Yes, but that's not a reason to make more work for ourselves. I like chocolate, too, but I'm not going to suggest we make our business a candy factory." Hadley shakes her head and all her blonde curls move around, mesmerizing me for a second.

Focus, Cooper.

"Good point, good point. The thing is, I'm hoping this won't be an imaginary business. I've been thinking for a while about opening a distillery on the farm."

Hadley narrows her eyes. "A distillery? This is the first I've heard of that. Lily's never said anything about opening a distillery."

"That's because I haven't told her yet. Haven't told anyone, actually. Other than Eddie McDonald, you're the only other person I've told." I'm hoping having Hadley think she's in on a secret will win me points somehow. It's unlikely, but I'm going to need to go for broke if I want her to help me.

"You haven't told anyone?" Hadley tilts her head. "Then how's this a better project idea than my salon one? We'd have to do so much work to get the information we need. Do you even know how to make whiskey?"

"Of course I do." Even I'm surprised by the indignation in my voice. "You've tasted my corn whiskey."

"That's moonshine, Cooper. It isn't the same thing."

"You'd be surprised how close it is, and I've already done plenty of the research myself into how it all would work."

Hadley regards me suspiciously. I know she doesn't trust me; I've given her all sorts of reasons not to. "Define 'research.'"

"Well, I've been making moonshine since I was fifteen."

"That doesn't count." Hadley rolls her eyes.

"Let me finish," I protest. "I've also been working at Eddie Mack's since I came back to Mint Springs. I'm down there a few days a week learning the business side of things. I've done my research on the setup I'd like and the legal stuff. We wouldn't be starting from scratch." I fold my hands on the top of the kitchen table. "At least consider it."

"You're serious?"

"As a heart attack."

"Then why haven't you told anyone else about this?"

It's a reasonable question, and one I have a ready answer to: *I'm afraid to.* Afraid of being told it's a dumb idea. Afraid of having my brothers poke holes in my plan or my research. I'm not the smart one, by any means. But Hadley's smart. Brilliant, even, when she sets her mind to it.

"I need a solid plan before I present it to them."

"And if we use your idea for our project then you'll have that?" Hadley doesn't look convinced.

"Yes, I'll have something more polished. And we'll get an A. I promise." I try to look sure.

"You can't guarantee that, Cooper."

"I can guarantee I'll work hard. This is important to me, Hadley." I pause, sure I'm digging my grave with this next part. "And I'll owe you."

This piques her interest.

"You'll owe me?" Those big blue eyes search my face, probably trying to catch me in a lie.

"Most certainly. And we can do fun research like whiskey tastings. Come on, it'll be way more interesting than thinking about a hair salon."

I can see her considering it, wavering a bit. "You can expect me to collect. You know that, right?"

"I wouldn't expect anything less, Hadley."

She chews a bit on that full bottom lip. "Fine. But you'd better bring your A-game, Cooper."

Oh, I'm bringing it.

9

Cooper

"What is that supposed to be, exactly?" I tilt my head. "Are we looking at it upside down?"

My brothers all roll their eyes, but not a one of them can answer my question. You would think one of us would be able to read these blueprints.

"Chance? Isn't this your area here? What the hell is that?"

"I'm not an architect, Cooper." He laughs. "We can have one of them explain the drawings. These aren't really important for us right now, anyway. We need to take a look at these renderings and see if those match what we're envisioning."

Charlie and Cade lean in, heads nearly touching. I stay where I am. I already know those pictures don't include what I'd like to see. That's no one's fault but mine, since I haven't bothered to tell any of my brothers even the first thing about my distillery dream.

"What's this building over here?" Charlie points to the edge of the giant piece of paper we're all assembled around.

"That should be the new offices for Lily." Chance taps his finger on the paper. "She's outgrown the barn already, and if the restaurant and events space are successful, she's going to need even more space. I'll keep an office in that building too, so I can collaborate with her."

"Is that what we're calling it now?" I can't resist the opportunity to tease Chance, not when he teed it up so perfectly.

He cuts his eyes over toward me. "Watch it, Coop. I'm gonna tell her you said that. You'll be without coffee for at least a week."

I frown. Living with Chance and Lily has definite drawbacks.

"When's Cooper's house supposed to be ready? I'd think you'd be anxious to be rid of him." Cade raises an eyebrow, and I think about giving him a shove. Complete maturity, that's me. Living in my newlywed little brother's house and still wrestling with the rest of my siblings at even the hint of a slight.

"It's coming along. Construction slowed down in the winter, but it should be back on track now. You should go take a look, especially if you're thinking you might want to build one too." Chance says it like it's no big deal. *Here little brother, have a house. I'll even build it for you.* He doesn't even look up from the plans. "Why don't you guys go over there now? We've got plenty of time to look at these, and we should talk about the details before we commit to any of this. Cade? Charlie? Y'all got those business plans yet? I want to be sure this isn't going to be a waste of all our time."

And Chance's money. I shut my mouth before it comes out, but we're all thinking it. Cade's at least coming into this with a business degree. Charlie doesn't have two nickels to rub together, but he's got plenty of restaurant experience. He knows how to run things, and he's got the confidence to do it. Me? I've got none of that. All of my jobs have been the kind you don't stay in for long—there'd be no reason. "Dead end" as my father so eloquently put it the last time I spoke to him. He'd had the same subdued reaction when I'd finally gotten up the courage to tell him there was no need to plan on attending my graduation ceremony all those years ago. No matter how hard I tried —retaking classes, choosing the easiest ones I could find, spending days in the Writing Center—I'd still come up short on my graduation requirements. My mother had done more of the appropriate hand wringing, worried about how her parenting had failed me again. Neither of them had offered me much else, though, and the humilia- tion of those calls had haunted me for a long time. All that time and money wasted. Cooper Allen—once consid- ered the golden boy, now most certainly nothing but a fuck up.

"Come on if y'all want to see it before supper. It'll be hard to look at anything in the dark." I motion for my youngest two brothers to follow me, and we pile into my truck. It's nothing fancy, but it works for Mint Springs and the farm. And I paid for it in cash, so I own it free and clear. I might have been working jobs with no future, but I wasn't stupid with my money. What little there was of it.

"Watch your elbow, Cade." We do not all fit nicely in the cab. My brothers jostle like they're third graders and not grown men.

"It's a five minute drive," I mutter under my breath, steering us up toward what will eventually be my house. I put the truck in park at the top of the hill and throw open the creaky driver's side door.

"Wow," Charlie says from somewhere behind me. "This

is a great spot. I don't think I've ever noticed the view from here."

It's not a section of the farm we spent much time on as kids. The entire farm parcel's just short of one hundred and fifty acres, and there's plenty of space out here we never really explored. We all did our fair share of running around, but none of my brothers spent much time here, where the pasture meets the pine forest. There's enough of a rise to feel like you're looking down on the pond, and from here you can see the mountains in the distance. In the morning the peaks'll sometimes be covered in fog and then the whole place gets this secret quality, like you're the only one alive, and the world's covered in mystery. It's quiet out here too. Far enough away from Cooper's house to give us both some privacy and close enough to the one place on this farm I remember the best.

"The old still used to be over there." I point to the pine trees. It was a few generations back, but deep in the forest you can still find the spot, if you know what you're looking for. When I was maybe twelve or thirteen, Grandpa showed it to me. It was an accident, really, him telling me the story when we came upon the clearing. We'd been checking the fence line on this far side, and it meant traipsing through the woods for a bit, trying to find the spots where the barbed wire had come down and needed repairing.

It had seemed almost magical to find this hidden place. And then to learn there had been an illegal moonshine still? I wasn't much into dragons or soldiers or cops and robbers, but I was very interested in this. My poor grandfather hadn't been able to keep up with all my questions. And my interest in the art and science of distilling was quickly more than he could handle. Not long after, he introduced me to Eddie, who seemed to know all about everything I wanted to learn.

Eddie even knew the Allen family recipe.

That right there's as close as I'm ever going to get to a legacy. As near as I'll ever be to touching something bigger. I like the idea that it's right outside my front door.

"I forgot there was a still." Cade's next to me now, taking in the view. "This is a good spot, Coop."

"Yeah," I agree. I was lucky Chance was amenable to letting me build here. He even gifted me five acres so I would own the house outright—not that I could ever sell it, anyway. To get out here you have to drive through the farm and we'd never allow that. And I'd never be able to let someone get so close to the clearing I know's a few feet into the trees.

"Come and see what's been done so far." I motion for my brothers to follow me. "It should start going up pretty fast here in the next couple of weeks."

We walk around what will eventually be my house. The foundation's been laid and the walls are starting to go up. Now that things are framed, it's starting to look like it'll eventually be something. Chance and Lily helped me decide on the specifics. Lily loved looking through house plans on the Internet, scouring *Southern Living* for the perfect little farmhouse to build here on my hill. She'd actually sighed when we found the plans for this one—not too big and not too small, with a great front porch for a couple of rocking chairs.

By the time we finish walking through the skeleton of my future home, the sun's starting to set. The oranges, fiery reds, and purples fan out over the mountains in the most spectacular show you've ever seen. Every sunset out here looks like a painting, almost too beautiful to be real.

"You have to put a hot tub out here for that alone," Charlie says, and Cade nods, both of them looking at the way the sun's sliding down behind the mountain peaks like it's the first time they've seen it.

"Not sure about the hot tub, but I've got big plans for the porch." I can picture myself sitting here at the end of a long day, glass of whiskey in my hand. Unfortunately, whenever I think about the future like this, I always include an element I'm certain is pure fantasy.

I always put Hadley sitting right beside me.

"Hadley'll like it. You brought her out here yet?" It's like Cade can read my mind, and Hadley popping in there is too much for him to resist.

"Of course not. Why would I bring Hadley out here?" I intend that to imply why *would I bring her anywhere?* But my brothers know better.

"You know why." The fading light does nothing to hide the smirk on Charlie's face.

"Can't say that I do." I keep my face pointed toward the sunset Hadley will never see.

"I don't understand why you both keep acting like you hate each other." Cade scuffs his boot in the dirt around the foundation.

"She isn't acting. Hadley hates me and that's the way it should be. We should get going. Don't want to be late for supper. Sadie and Mae'll be unhappy if the food gets cold." That's the understatement of the year. Our great aunts do not tolerate late to dinner. Ever. And since they've been slaving over a hot stove to cook for all of us, I don't want to push my luck. I'm no chef, and I rely on my spinster aunts to keep me in cornbread.

"I don't understand what happened with the two of you. That summer you both seemed..." Charlie trails off but Cade has no trouble picking up where he left off.

"Like cats in heat?"

I give him a menacing glare he most likely can't see in the waning light. "It isn't anyone's business what happened." How can I explain to Charlie and Cade that no matter how perfect that summer was, Hadley Crawford was never going to be mine? Not for real and not for long. I did her a favor by cutting her loose. It's too bad she didn't originally see it for what it was. "Just get in the truck."

We ride in silence all the way back to Mae and Sadie's house, pulling up in time to see Chance and Lily walking over from theirs. They've fixed up my grandpa's old house, the one he originally built for his own family—my grandma and my father. Sadie and Mae live next door. Or next door in farm terms. You can see their house from Chance and Lily's, but it's far enough away for everyone to get a little privacy. That's how my grandpa planned it when he convinced his sisters to live here. It's the same thing Chance said to me when he suggested making this compound we're making now. Close enough to help each other but far enough apart not to be in each other's business.

Yeah, right.

I can feel Charlie and Cade mulling over my "business" as we get out of the truck and walk up the porch steps. I notice a loose board and make a mental note to come over tomorrow to nail it down. Chance and I try our best to make sure problems at Mae and Sadie's are solved before they even notice. In return, they give us the best home-cooked meals you can imagine and that kind of smothering love you can only get from family.

Tonight, I walk into a house that smells of Mae's pot roast. A heaping bowl of mashed potatoes is already sitting on the table. Sadie's pulling rolls out of the oven, her arms stuffed into a pair of enormous oven mitts, and Mae's finishing up whatever she's got on the stove.

"You boys hurry and wash up! Supper'll be ready in five," Mae yells over her shoulder, and we all scatter to various sinks to make sure we get all the day's filth and grit off our hands. There are no dirty hands tolerated at Sadie and Mae's table. They may not have any children of their own, but when we were here in the summers, they made sure we were raised right. *Put on a shirt; take off that hat; put that napkin in your lap, young man.* They wanted civilized, and we managed to pull that off for a few hours every evening.

"It smells delicious," I tell Mae while I wash my hands at the kitchen sink, making sure to get under my fingernails.

"Well, there's none of your cornbread, but I've had that roast in the oven all day just for you, Cooper." Mae gives me a wink. I am more than spoiled here, even more so than I was as a kid, if that's possible. Mae always tried to act like it wasn't true, but I'm her favorite. "Use those muscles to put these beans on the table." She hands me a steaming bowl of green beans, a huge pat of butter starting to melt on top.

Chance and Lily are already at the table putting out the silverware and napkins. Lily looks up at me as I lean over to set the bowl down. "You show them the house?"

"Yeah."

"And?" Lily cocks her head, her shiny brown waves sliding with the movement.

"And they agree I picked the best spot."

Cade chooses that minute to plop into his seat. It doesn't escape anyone's notice that he makes sure he puts the rolls he's carrying directly in front of him. "Plenty of great spots left."

Charlie looks around, sees we're all seated, and brings up the subject I know he's been dying to talk about for the last thirty minutes. "Told Cooper Hadley's going to love it."

Lily snorts. "I don't think we need to worry about Hadley moving in with Cooper any time soon." She takes a heaping spoonful of glazed carrots and passes the bowl to me. "She *is* worried about being partnered with you in that class, though."

The entire room goes quiet. Only Chance keeps right on chewing.

"What class?" Cade asks.

"The marketing class." Lily's brown eyes search the other faces at the table. "The one he needs to graduate."

"Graduate?" Mae's voice shakes a little.

I look down at my plate.

"He's been taking classes online..." Lily looks at Chance. "Do they really not know about this?"

Chance shrugs. He barely knows anything about it either, but he's not about to tell anyone else this.

"College," Mae says, and I swear her eyes are misty. "Cooper Allen, I'm thrilled."

"Don't get too excited," I caution. "I have to get through this class first."

"I'm sure you'll do well." Mae's confidence in me gives me a little boost, almost enough to make me forget about the giant Hadley-shaped obstacle in front of me. "Now tell us all about it."

10

Hadley

"Hadley Crawford, is that you?"

I freeze, the wonky front wheel of my shopping cart spinning around uselessly. Neither one of us is going to be able to roll out of here anytime soon.

Molly Mitchell—formerly Molly Eagan—wheels her cart directly in front of mine, blocking my way forward in the aisle. Trapped in the Piggly Wiggly with the nosiest girl from Mint Springs Elementary—I wouldn't expect anything less from an early Sunday morning.

"I thought that might be you. I'd recognize that hair anywhere. And you always managed to stay so slim." Molly's green eyes rake over me with just a hint of hostility. After four children in close succession, Molly's a little chubby around the middle. She was always worried about her weight growing up, constantly talking about the current fad diet she was hoping would be her magic bullet. She tugs at the front of her sparkly, monogrammed T-shirt.

"Well, you were right. It's me. Trying to get a little grocery shopping done." I nod at my half-full cart.

"This would be the time to do it, what with everyone else at church." It would be more of a dig if Molly wasn't also standing in the supermarket instead of planted in the front pew of Mint Springs Methodist. "Don't tell anyone we're skipping today," she whispers conspiratorially. "Brad's having some people over for a barbecue this afternoon, and between the kids and my work I could *not* find time to get organized."

Bradley Mitchell. Former football tight end and student body president. Smart, kind, helpful. Current husband to Molly and father to four small, cherubic children all usually dressed in matching smocked outfits from Molly's in-home business, Smock It to Me. Also my former high school boyfriend who could not compete with the magic that was Cooper Allen.

Molly swooped in as soon as Bradley and I were kaput, soothing his ego and hurt feelings enough to have her attached to his hip for four years in college and immediately walking down the aisle after they graduated. Not that I can blame her; Bradley Mitchell was a catch, especially around here. Now he's working some kind of finance job, commuting between here and Chattanooga, making enough to have just built Molly her dream house.

"Brad's been running that smoker nonstop trying to get ready for today. He's got a bunch of guys coming from work —you know I can't have all those other wives over without making my famous potato salad. And there's never enough cold drinks, so I had to do another grocery run." Molly's cart's full of cans of soda. When she notices me pausing over all the drink mixers, she giggles a little self-consciously. "And there'll be *other* drinks, obviously. It is a party, after all."

"Of course." I try to move my cart a little to hint at my

intention to get on with my shopping. "It sounds lovely. And the weather's supposed to be great." A nice, sunny, early spring day. Molly's lucked out not to get one of the wet, cold afternoons February can serve up around here.

"I'm sure people'll be inside the house anyway. That's why we went ahead and planned it for now instead of waiting until later. Brad loves to show off that house. And it's good incentive for some of the up-and-coming guys. You know, lets them see what's possible with hard work and dedication." Molly pulls on the strap of her purse absent-mindedly. "What's new with you?"

"Nothing, really." I try to keep my voice light, unbothered. Having nothing to report is the best way to be around here. "Still working at Hot House, trying to help people live their prettiest lives."

Molly smiles at this. "How's things with Cooper?" It's the question I'm sure she's been dying to ask.

"With Cooper?" I act genuinely perplexed. "What do you mean?"

"I thought... Well, people have seen you with Cooper lately, and I thought that might mean..." Molly waits for me to pick up where she left off, desperate for me to fill in the blanks.

"Oh, no. There's nothing between me and Cooper." I'm starting to sound like a broken record with all the Cooper denials I've had to issue lately. Have one cup of coffee and suddenly you're on track for a white dress and a car full of baby seats.

"I'm sorry to hear that. I know how crazy you used to be about him."

"*Used to be*," I reassure her. "Turns out he wasn't who I thought he was." That should be enough to placate Molly into letting me finish my shopping. I wrap my hands tightly around the cart handles. "Good seeing you."

"You, too," Molly says, still not moving. "I was really hoping things would work out between you and Cooper. Brad and I do so want you to end up happy."

I don't think it even occurs to Molly that I might find her concern offensive. And the way she said it, like we were in some Disney princess movie and I needed rescuing? No, thank you. I'm perfectly happy the way I am, and I'm about to tell her that when she interrupts my thoughts.

"The dating pool around here is, well, a little shallow." She whispers that last part, like the lack of eligible men our age in Mint Springs needs to be kept just among us. I think most everyone knows this town isn't a Mecca for bachelors worth shaving your legs. No need to keep your voice down. "You know what? You should come to our barbecue. There'll be a handful of single guys from Brad's office. Chattanooga boys. And Brad would love to see you."

I doubt that last part, but I'm intrigued by the promise of an afternoon with new people. Sure, I'll have to deal with whatever story Molly wants to tell about how we know each other, but I can survive that. And I do like Molly's potato salad.

"I'll think about it. Thanks for the invitation." I hear myself saying as I wave goodbye to Molly and finish the rest of my shopping. I even find myself putting an extra dozen eggs in my cart in case the mood to make deviled eggs strikes me and I need to not show up empty-handed. A barbecue at Molly and Brad's might be the perfect way to spend a Sunday afternoon.

A party at Molly and Brad's turns out to be a horrendous way to spend an afternoon. The promise of perfect weather doesn't hold, but that's the least of my worries. From the moment I walk in the front door—an enormous, grand entrance kind of thing—I'm paraded around by Molly and introduced as Brad's ex. That was a flex I hadn't anticipated: Molly's story of finding Brad and living happily ever after requiring me to be the girl he ultimately decided couldn't hold a candle to her. Luckily, I've taken pains today to look my best. Had I shown up in cutoffs and a T-shirt, this back-story reveal would hurt quite a bit more.

"Here." Bradley hands me a glass. "I'm going to assume you still like whiskey."

"I do, thank you." I take the drink he offers and let the burn of the liquor mentally transport me off this back porch and into my living room.

"Sorry about Molly. She gets a little insecure. I told her to tone it down. It's a wonder you haven't already run off." Brad takes a sip from his drink and looks out over the giant backyard.

"She doesn't have anything to be insecure about." I look at Brad's profile. He's still handsome, even if his face has filled out a bit over the years. "She's got a successful business, good kids, a beautiful house, and a handsome husband. She was trying to be kind when she invited me." And leaving before I've been here thirty minutes would look rude. I am, however, counting those minutes down.

"Thanks for the handsome part," Brad says, giving me a little tip of his head, and I note he's still got a full head of hair. There's another thing for Molly to be happy about. "I think when you show up"—he gives me a quick glance—"looking like that, all that old stuff comes back up. Thanks for being a good sport."

"I'm not here to steal Molly's husband," I joke. I don't think I could, even if I wanted to. I've seen the way Brad looks at Molly.

Brad leans on the porch railing. He's dressed in what I assume he wears to work on casual Fridays—pressed khaki pants and a golf shirt. "What do you think of the house? It's obnoxious, isn't it?"

"Maybe a little, but you like it, right?" I do not want to get into a discussion of the ostentatiousness of this house as I stand on its expansive porch with its owner.

"Molly loves it; that's the only thing I care about." Brad finishes his drink and stands up straight. "You want to come back inside? I'd have thought you'd want to stay dry." He holds his free hand out and lets a little of the drizzle land there.

"I'll come in in a bit. I might need five more minutes."

"Suit yourself. Good stuff's in the liquor cabinet. Help yourself once you're ready." The screen door closes behind him, and I take one more deep breath.

Once my glass is empty, I have a decision to make. I can either say my goodbyes and leave, or I can have another drink. Either way, I have to go back inside this sprawling McMansion. I steel myself and manage to slip back in without attracting too much attention. My search for the liquor cabinet leads me to what I assume must be Brad's study. There's a dark wooden desk—the kind better suited to the White House than Bradley Mitchell's butt—and a giant bookcase full of leather-bound books. This is obviously for show as well, but I pull one of them down and thumb through it anyway.

"You lost too?"

The voice startles me and I drop the book on the floor,

which narrowly misses my foot and bounces open on the rug.

"Sorry, I didn't mean to scare you." The apology comes from a man standing in the doorway. He's tall, blond, and staring at me as I try to collect myself.

"I didn't expect to see anyone else," I explain, trying to pick up the book as gracefully as possible. "I was looking for the liquor cabinet and got distracted. Brad said I could get myself a drink."

"You got distracted by..." He moves close enough to read the spine of the book I'm trying to put back on the shelf. He's close enough now that I can smell the woodsy scent of his aftershave. "*Moby Dick*?"

I tilt back a bit to look him full in the face. He's handsome, with a strong jaw and blue eyes. Handsome enough to have me stuttering a bit. "I...I wasn't really reading it. I was... Well, frankly I was wondering if these were actually real books." I let the arm closest to the bookshelf flail wildly.

"Well, are they?" I focus on his lips.

"Are they what?"

He laughs, and the sound is mesmerizing. "Are they real books?"

"Oh, yes, I think so. At least that one is. I didn't get a chance to really check it out before you came in, compare it against what I remember from the story." I smooth the front of my dress with my palms.

"You've read *Moby Dick*?"

"Of course. Hasn't everybody? It's a classic." I blink at this handsome stranger, waiting for his answer.

"I doubt everybody has. It may be a classic, but it's boring. And too long. But that's just my opinion. I'm Ryan, by the way." He stretches out a hand.

"Hadley." I put my own hand out, and he takes it firmly but gently. I nearly swoon. "Very nice to meet you."

"Now, where's that liquor cabinet? What are you drinking?"

We end up sitting in the overstuffed leather chairs Brad has in this room. It really does look like the kind of room a kid decorated to fit the idea of an office. There are a few framed photos of Molly and the kids, but other than that it could be a movie set. I doubt Brad does any actual work in here.

"So how do you know Brad and Molly?" I brace myself for the explanation I'll have to give about my connection to our hosts.

"I work with Brad."

"Ah, one of the guys from the Chattanooga office." I congratulate myself on being able to form a coherent sentence.

"Yes, I'm not from there originally, but I live there now." Ryan sips on his drink. "You were right about this whiskey."

"Where're you from then?" More points to me for small talk. He doesn't have an accent I can place, and Ryan isn't from around here. I'd know if a man like this had been anywhere near Mint Springs.

"California. I came to Chattanooga for college and liked it so much I stayed." His smile's easy, and I'm enjoying this impromptu cocktail party more than I should.

"You chose Tennessee over California?" I can't hide my surprise.

"Sure. California's nice, but the South's got a lot to offer: the people are nice, there's plenty to do, the women are beautiful." He raises one eyebrow a bit at this last part, glancing at my legs.

My cheeks pink up, and I have to pretend to be very interested in my drink to hide my smile.

I don't bother to hide it on Monday, however, when Ryan crosses state lines again and waltzes into Hot House Flowers just as I'm finishing up a cut and color on Carol Anne Simmons.

"I was not at all in the neighborhood and was hoping I could take you to lunch."

Swoon.

11

Cooper

"You're going to have to work faster than that if we're going to be finished before supper."

"Me?" I'm incredulous. "I hope that's you over there talking to yourself, Charlie." I make like I'm handing him the post-hole digger. "We can switch jobs any time you like."

Putting this fence back together's back-breaking work. Worse than the physical exertion of it is the knowledge it'll never actually be finished. Fences constantly need repairing, and there's no shortage of fences on this farm. Today we're moving along the northernmost part of the property, trying to make sure all the barbed wire is where it's supposed to be. It isn't, of course, because it never is, so Charlie and I are moving slowly along the property line trying to fix what we can in these last hours of daylight.

"You know what would be great to do with this little piece of land right here?" Charlie asks, ignoring my offer of the digger.

"Fix the rest of the fence?" I wipe my brow. It's not even a hot day, and I'm sweating through my shirt.

Charlie rolls his eyes. "Okay, yes, that, but also think about a vegetable garden."

"A what? Why?"

"For the restaurant. If we're serious about doing this, we should do it right. Grow as much of the produce as we can here. Maybe even go back to raising some of our own animals. We could have chickens, pigs—"

"Whoa, slow down there. Do you even know how to plant a garden? Have you ever grown anything?" I don't imagine Charlie's been spending the last few years working on his little homestead.

Charlie scowls. "As a matter of fact, I do know how to plant a garden. The last place I worked was completely farm to table. We had a rooftop garden right there in the middle of downtown Atlanta. I helped out a lot. I'm not an expert, exactly, but I can grow a few things."

I give Charlie a shrug. Maybe he does know what he's talking about.

"We could talk to Matt over at the nursery. That'd be a good place to start with the garden, I think. Not sure about the pigs..." Charlie's in his own little world now, not even pretending to care about the fence.

"Wait a second. Stopping by Sullivan's to buy a few plants is one thing. Pigs is a completely different subject." I thrust the digger into the spot where the next post needs to go with a grunt. "And you can't have animals running around without a fence."

"I know, I know. But Sadie and Mae have chickens. We'd do that on a larger scale. And we used to have horses and cows—pigs too, remember?"

"Oh, I remember. And I also remember having to pull cows out of the river, and chasing escaped pigs all summer. I recall Grandpa cussing quite a bit about all of that. Are you ready with the fencepost or not?"

"Calm down." Charlie lugs one of the wooden posts from the back of the truck and brings it over. "I just wanted you to think about it. We're not doing it tomorrow."

"Fine."

We wrestle the post into the hole.

"Let's do two more and then call it a day. I'll come back out tomorrow to finish up." I'm trying my best to make the work I do last out here. Digging the holes deep for the fenceposts, reinforcing them. It might not make a bit of difference, though, if Charlie's grand plans get in the way of the basics.

Charlie nods. "Sounds good." He hesitates for a second. "You know, you could come up with something you wanted to do."

"Who says I haven't?" I regret it as soon as it's out of my mouth.

"*You* do, or at least it seems that way. You've never told me about anything you want to do around here. I mean, you're doing plenty, and we all appreciate it, but where's the thing that'll make you excited to get out of bed in the morning? If you've got something, why don't you tell the rest of us?"

I shrug, try to play it off as me running my mouth. "Maybe I will." *Soon*. I turn back to the fence and the never-ending line of broken and crooked fenceposts. "But we've got to finish this first."

After dinner, all I want to do is sit on the front porch and enjoy a glass of whiskey. I'm amassing quite the collection now, trying a little bit of everything to see if I can explain the "flavor profiles." That's an Eddie idea, although I never would have thought he'd know anything about that. When I'd laughed, he'd set me straight real quick. *You want to be taken serious with this, then you'd best start acting serious, Cooper.* He hadn't had to tell me twice. He'd recommended a few books and I've taken a look, but since reading's never been my cup of tea, I found a few podcasts to get some the same information. I'm about to press play on one when Chance joins me out on the porch. It's his house, after all, so I act reasonable and pull my headphones from my ears.

"Sorry, I didn't realize you were doing something." He looks at the earbuds in my hand.

"I'm not," I lie. No reason to make things uncomfortable, and I don't have any intention of starting a conversation about what I'm listening to. I'm not ready.

"Thought I might join you out here for a bit, if that's okay." Chance settles himself on the step next to me. "What're you drinking?"

"Grab a glass and I'll give you some." It is literally the least I can do.

When Chance comes back, I pour him two fingers of what is fast becoming my favorite whiskey in the entire world. This week, at least. I'm finding some really delicious whiskey now that I'm doing so much research.

The surprised noise Chance makes with his first sip confirms my own initial feelings.

"It's good, right? And sort of local. It's made in Georgia. I've got another one from Nashville and..." I lean back a bit to grab the third bottle I've brought with me. "This one's Chattanooga. All close."

"You drinking three bottles of whiskey tonight?" Chance raises an eyebrow.

"No," I protest. "I'm *tasting* three whiskeys tonight."

"Fancy." Chance tips the entirety of his glass back in one gulp.

"No, no!" My raised voice seems even louder out here in the dark. "You have to sip it, Chance. Actually, you should kind of chew it, try to make the aftertaste last as long as possible."

Chance regards me skeptically. "You're serious?"

"Yes. This isn't about trying to drink as much as possible; it's about really understanding the flavors." I pour him another, much smaller, glass. "This time, sort of roll it around in your mouth. Just a tiny sip, though. In a second we'll add a little water or an ice cube, see how that changes things."

Chance's face changes as he moves the liquor around in his mouth. I almost expect him to close his eyes. After he swallows he gives his lips a few smacks.

"See?" I prod. "Not at all like drinking at Bootlegger."

"You're right. What's the name of this one?"

I hand him the bottle. "These tonight are all rye whiskeys. Spicy. This one's got a pretty good bit of caramel in the finish. What do you think?"

"I think I need a little more," Chance jokes and then takes another sip. "Where'd you even get these?"

"You'd be surprised what old Mr. Sims can get if you ask nicely. And some of these are driving distance away." I don't tell Chance about my plans to visit all these distilleries. It's too soon to start talking about all that, even if the wheels in my head are already turning so fast I'm surprised he can't smell the burning rubber.

"Tasting in the dark isn't the best idea, though. It's difficult to really see the color, but I think it helps me to really smell and taste the whiskey. I'm not relying on my eyes. And

I like sitting out here at night when I can." I take a big breath of the country air.

"It's a little chilly out here tonight, though. You want to move this party inside? I bet Lily'd like your fancy whiskey tasting." Chance stands and starts toward the door.

"I'm amenable to that so long as I'm not intruding on your private time." I swirl the liquor around in my glass.

"Is that a euphemism?" Chance laughs. "We get plenty of 'private time.' Come on in the house, or at least let's get jackets."

"I do appreciate you and Lily letting me live here. I know that probably isn't how you imagined starting out married life—with your idiot big brother at the kitchen table every morning." I try to pretend it's a joke, but Chance knows me, knows there's more than a grain of truth in there.

"You're not an idiot, and we're happy to have you. Your house'll be finished soon and then we'll all miss being packed in together like this. And we'd never get that fence fixed without you, so I guess we can put up with the loud way you slurp your cereal."

"I don't slurp."

"You do. But it's fine, Cooper. Come inside and show Lily your collection. I'll help you carry some of it." Chance reaches out his hand, and I put one of the bottles in it. There's no way I could lug all of this inside in one trip so I rely on my brother. Again.

But eventually I'm going to be able to stand on my own.

12

Hadley

"You don't think it'll be too light?"

"No, I'm sure you're going to love it. And it'll let you go a bit longer in between appointments. As much as I love visiting with you, I know you hate being stuck in the chair for hours." I smile at the woman in the mirror. I'll actually be a little sad to see less of Laney King. She's one of the few people I know who's had the chance to leave Mint Springs but then willingly came back. Lily's another, but she hadn't been gone for long. Laney, on the other hand, had lived an entire life out from under the small-town expectations of Mint Springs.

"If there's anyone I'd trust to tell me the truth about my hair it's you, Hadley. I cannot believe how much gray has come in here in this one little patch." Laney lifts her hands out from under the smock I've got on her and pulls a bit at the hair framing her face. "I mean, if it could all come in like Bonnie Raitt, I'd be happy. A cool stripe right down the front here, maybe? But, of course, it's not going to do that and I'm not ready to look...old." She sighs. "I put myself in your capable hands."

"I promise to take care of you." That's a promise I can easily keep here at Hot House Flowers. I give the customer what they want. "Let me go and mix up your color, and we'll get you looking seventeen again. Can I get you a magazine?"

"If you can get me looking seventeen again, I'll pay you double. Matt would fall on the floor if seventeen-year-old me came waltzing back into the house tonight." Laney gets a kind of wistful look on her face for a second. "Although I wouldn't go back to seventeen today if I had to navigate all the things Trey's having to."

"Matt's boy's having trouble?" This is one of the unexpected parts of the job I hadn't given my mother and grandmother enough credit for. Every hairdresser has to be a therapist from time to time. Marriages, divorces—all the family drama comes out in the chair. People trust me with information they'd never tell their very best friend.

"Not trouble, exactly." Laney's mouth twists a bit. "He's with his mother most of the time, so I don't think Matt always gets the full story on school. And Trey's smart, but high school's got a different set of expectations, and it turns out he's got some learning challenges. Go ahead and mix the color, and I'll tell you about it." Laney shoos me away with her hand. "This is going to take more than a minute."

I scurry over to the supply closet and start combining the chemicals I'll need to make Laney King into the prom queen. Not that she needs much help. She might be in her forties, but Laney always looks like she's glowing. I'm not sure if that's because she's an artist or because she's madly in love with Matt Sullivan. Their love story is the kind that makes me believe in happily ever afters for real. They loved each other in high school, but went off to pursue their own dreams. They never forgot about each other, though, and when Laney had to come home to care for her sick mother, Matt was already back here. They'd both had the success they wanted, but it turned out they still wanted each other. Like missing pieces. I'm hoping there's not trouble in paradise.

I roll the cart over, making sure I've got all the supplies I need for Laney's supermodel hair. "Alright, resume," I joke as I start to dab the cream around Laney's hairline.

"Well, Trey's never been a superstar at school. I don't think he'd mind me telling you this. He's always been like Matt—more interested in baseball than anything else. I don't think Matt's ex-wife had considered there might be anything going on other than a little laziness; I know Matt hadn't. This year, though, it really became apparent something wasn't right."

I watch her talk, noticing the concern in her voice for Trey. He's not technically her stepson, but you can tell she worries about him anyway.

"I'm afraid to even guess," I say, moving along Laney's scalp with the comb and my paintbrush. Already her hair is sticking out in ways only fit to be seen by other women at the beauty salon.

"We were all concerned, and there were all these meetings with teachers and administrators. It looked like Trey wasn't going to be able to get his grades up enough to play ball, which was bad, but then we realized he was actually failing several classes. Failing! Matt about died." Laney shakes her head, and I have to make sure I stay out of the line of fire in case any of the dye I'm slathering her with decides to splatter.

"But then one of the resource teachers at school noticed something we had all kind of been overlooking."

"What?" I'm exceptionally invested in this story, not only because Trey Sullivan seems like the sweetest kid when he's here in the summers working at his father's garden supply store, but also because I cannot imagine the kind of thing that would make a boy like that turn into a juvenile delinquent, which I'm pretty sure is where this story's going.

"Trey can barely read."

My surprised stare meets Laney's in the mirror. "He can't *read*? How is that possible? He's sixteen or something!"

"Exactly! It seems impossible, but it's true. He never liked to read, and he had some trouble when he was younger, but somehow he's managed to get through all of these years of school. He slipped through the cracks. He can *read*, but he has trouble using that as the primary way he accesses information. It's slow, and his comprehension isn't what it should be."

"But wouldn't someone have noticed? How in the world did he do his homework? Take tests?" I pull one of the aluminum foil sheets loose from the pile in front of me and start Laney's highlights.

"He'd figured out little workarounds, ways to get the information without really reading the textbook. For smaller chunks of text he's fine, but it takes him forever. He's been convincing girls to read assignments to him and getting things explained by his baseball buddies. We were all flabbergasted. And then they did some tests, and Trey has *dyslexia*. He's dyslexic, and no one figured it out until now." Laney's eyes are wet with the start of a good cry. "I'm sorry. I just think about how stressful school must have been for him all this time and that he did it all alone, thinking he was dumb or something."

I reach for a tissue from the box I keep at my station. "Don't you dare worry about crying in here. That story would make anyone tear up." I hand Laney the tissue and blink away my own tears. "Poor Trey."

"Yes! And they have all these things now to help him, but think if we'd caught this sooner. He could have been getting extra tutoring and using audiobooks the entire time. He is a junior, for Pete's sake! He struggled for so long for no reason." Laney dabs her eyes with a tissue.

"The important thing is y'all figured it out, Laney."

"I know, but we all feel so guilty and Matt's furious with the school for not saying anything sooner—for not picking up on the clues. That's really a lot of misplaced anger at himself, though. The school made some mistakes, sure, but Matt's really beating himself up over it. You try to do right by your child, and then you see how badly that can get screwed up."

I'm unsure of what to say. I'm not a mom—not even close—but I understand how fiercely you can love your family. I know how it feels to try to do what's best for them, even if it might not be best for you.

"Matt can't think... If even the teachers didn't figure it out..." I know my protestations won't change the way Matt and Laney feel about missing something that was happening in their child's life.

"Apparently it happens all the time. Kids don't want to tell everyone their problems. And Trey figured it out well enough until the workload got to be too much. I can't imagine. And Matt's ex-wife is so upset. The silver lining is getting Trey all squared away, of course, but the grownups are having a hard time figuring out what to do next."

I think about my conversation with Laney all the way home. I'm still thinking about it when Lily stops by for a drink. She's changed out of her work clothes, but she's still crusted in paint. It clings to the fine hairs on her forearms and flakes off her fingers.

"What if we had decided to go out?" I ask, giving Lily the onceover. I already know the answer. Lily loves refinishing furniture. Can hardly tear herself away from the painting she so rarely gets to do now that her business is more interior design. She loves that too, of course; Lily's ended up with her dream job and working with her dream man. We should all be so lucky.

"I could have gone out like this," she protests. "It's not like I'm trying to impress anyone."

"But *I* might be. I can't go around looking like ten miles of bad road, Lily. People will see us together and think I think it's acceptable to go out in public..." I wave my hand in her direction. "Like that."

Lily laughs. Admittedly, she still looks pretty cute. She can't help it; she'd look great in a paper sack with her face done up like one of those street urchins from the movie *Oliver*. "You afraid your new beau will surprise us and discover you in your off-duty clothes, Hadley?"

I scowl. "Off-duty" is what Lily calls my casual clothes. I make a point out of dressing for the occasion, even if there's no discernible occasion. It is better to be overdressed than underdressed. Everyone knows that. Reese Witherspoon says it all the time. Being well-dressed is a form of politeness. Ask around. And even if it sometimes takes me the better part of the day to end up looking like I woke up this way, well, that's my business.

"Oh, hush." I can't control the smile that's overtaking my lips. "And he's not my beau, Scarlett O'Hara. Not yet."

"Not yet, eh?" Lily goes ahead and makes herself comfortable on the couch. "I'm going to need to hear all about him. I assume you've got wine."

"Of course I do." I nearly skip to the kitchen to get the bottle of white I've got chilling in the fridge and two wine glasses. The cork makes a satisfying *pop* as I pull it from the bottle. "He's *perfect*, Lily," I yell into the living room.

"Perfect?" she asks as she takes her glass of wine from me. "I've heard that before."

I give Lily a look I hope qualifies as "withering." "I hope you aren't referring to your brother-in-law."

"Oh, I was talking about Cooper. Just don't want you to give this Ryan person too much of the rose-colored glasses treatment." Lily takes a sip of her wine. "Not that Cooper doesn't have his strong points."

I fake gag. Maturity isn't easy with me when it comes to Cooper. "I was blinded by his handsomeness. And I was also a kid. Don't forget that part." It's the defense I tell myself whenever I wonder how I had been so madly in love with Cooper Allen.

"He is nice to look at. I mean, he's no Chance, but he's okay." Lily smiles. "I do wish you and Cooper could call a truce. It looked like you were getting along for a minute there. When I came back from Chicago, you didn't want to rip each other's eyes out."

Ah, yes. That in-between time when Cooper started to act like the boy I remembered. His brother had been desperate to get Lily back, and Cooper had been the best brother he could be. I was missing my friend and worried about her, and Cooper had stepped into the void. He'd been supportive and caring, always ready with a joke to cheer me up, and we'd been forced to spend time together as Chance worked on his plan to convince Lily to move permanently back to Mint Springs. As soon as she was back, though, Cooper reverted to his old ways. If anything, he'd gotten even more annoying since. I had started to let my guard down with him and got enough of a singe to remember the first time he hurt me. I'm not about to get burned again.

"That was short-lived and ill-advised." I try to keep from pouting, but Lily's laugh tells me I've failed. "What? I should have known better. For some reason, Cooper really lives to get me riled up." Even now, just thinking about the ways he's tried to bother me has me bristling.

"I don't know why he's like that with you. He really can be a very nice guy. You know—you've seen the other side of Cooper."

"I have, but it was brief and fleeting." I clink my glass with Lily's. "But here's to this next one remaining as advertised."

"I hope he turns out to be everything you're hoping." Lily sips a bit more wine. "Before we completely forget about Cooper for the night, how's your class going?"

"As well as expected, I guess. I think we've got an idea for the big project, but I'm not entirely sold." I know Cooper doesn't want me telling Lily all about his big idea, so I don't give details, but I'm exasperated enough with him so far that I throw him under the bus a little. "It's something Cooper wants to do, but I don't know how serious he is."

"Why do you say that? At home he's working more than I've ever seen."

"On things for this class? I find that hard to believe. I've been sending him loads of articles but he never responds to any of my emails. I don't think he even reads any of them." I let my back relax into the couch cushions. Talking about Cooper has me sitting ramrod straight.

"He's not much of a reader. Never really has been, but he gets the work done, I think. I wouldn't worry too much about that. Now, when are you going out with Ryan again? Any big plans?"

Lily might be ready to leave the Cooper conversation, but my talk with Laney from earlier pokes just enough at me to ask one more question. "Cooper can read, can't he?"

Lily guffaws. "Of course he can, Hadley. There's nothing wrong with him. He isn't a great student, that's all." She gives me a look. "Can't read? You'd better hope I never tell him you asked that."

"He probably wouldn't care, anyway," I counter. "He'd probably have some smartass response ready for me before I even finished talking."

"Maybe." Lily finishes her wine. "Should we bring the bottle out here? And get dinner? We could make it a girls' night in kind of thing."

"Sure." I go back into the kitchen to grab the wine and get ready to try to forget all about Cooper Allen.

13

Cooper

"Why are you wearing that fancy shirt? It's only gonna get ruined if we have to move the mash today. You got a date or something after this?" Eddie almost scowls at the plaid button down I'm wearing.

"I don't have a date. What's wrong with wearing a shirt with buttons every now and again?" I glance at Eddie's grubby T-shirt and overalls ensemble. "Might help you out in the lady department if you spruced it up a bit every now and then."

Now Eddie really *does* scowl, the kind of expression that lets me know I'm in for it. "Firstly, I don't think I need any advice from the likes of you about how to impress women." He raises an eyebrow. "I do fine on that account, and the evidence plainly shows it. Secondly, how impressive is that shirt of yours going to be once it smells like wet corn? I imagine it'll look pretty different before we get done here today. And overalls are extremely practical." He goes back to counting the money in the till. As usual, there isn't much, but Eddie doesn't care nearly as much about making money as he does about making moonshine.

"Fine, fine." I raise my hands in surrender. "Your regular uniform is a winner." I do frequently envy Eddie's front pocket.

"I had years of the Army telling me how to dress, making me polish my shoes. I'm done with that. If you want to spend the day being uncomfortable that's your business."

"I'm not uncomfor—"

The tinkle of the bell over the door interrupts me. As Eddie and I both turn to look, the front of the store floods with light and in walks Hadley Crawford. Between the flowing blonde hair and the blinding light, I've never seen anything more angelic. She basically floats toward us, her long legs gliding along the floor.

"What in the—" Eddie looks at Hadley and then at me, his mouth turning down. "No reason, huh? Cooper Allen, you'd better not have ruined my day."

I try to wipe the stupid off my face. "'Course not. I invited Hadley to get the ten-cent tour. We're supposed to be working on a project together."

"A project?" Eddie harrumphs. "I've heard that before."

"Seriously, for that marketing class I told you about." I try to telegraph a million reminders to Eddie. I've told him about school, about my plans for the distillery, about my need to use the class to get my ducks in a row. I've left out the part about Hadley, but he's a smart man. He can connect the dots. Unfortunately, he connects them in a way that immediately gets my hackles raised.

"That's how you're planning on getting your business plan together?"

Luckily, Hadley's close enough now to inspire me to keep my mouth shut. I can explain the situation to Eddie later. I didn't orchestrate anything here; I'm making the best of a bad situation. I'm with Hadley because we have no choice, not that Eddie will believe that, I'm sure.

"I'm a little early." Hadley's eyes flit between Eddie's face and mine. "I hope that's okay." She extends one of her hands and presents it to Eddie, the creamy skin of her arms on full display as her arm stretches toward him. "I'm Hadley."

Eddie gives me one more scathing look before shaking Hadley's hand. "Pleased to meet you. Cooper didn't tell me you were coming by."

"Oh!" Hadley's mouth fixes itself into a startled *o* and her eyes widen. "I hope it's okay that I'm here. I thought Cooper would have mentioned his invitation to you in advance." Now I've got two people looking at me with disappointment.

"I was just getting to that before you came in." I rub my palms together. "I'm hoping to convince Hadley that my distillery idea is a good one for our project. I was going to give her a little taste of what I'm thinking today. Let her see the process."

"And you thought showing her this operation here would inspire her to love all things moonshine?" Eddie's brow furrows. "Thought you were smart, but this might make me reconsider that assessment."

"I like moonshine," Hadley interjects, and Eddie turns toward her.

"You do?"

"Of course I do. I prefer whiskey, but I can appreciate anything. I assume you think your moonshine is good?" Her question hits Eddie right in the chest.

"Good?" he sputters. "I'll have you know the moonshine we make here is the best in the world—the best you'll ever taste, young lady."

"Then I'm looking forward to learning all about it." Hadley gives him one of her smiles, and Eddie thaws a bit.

That's my girl, I think before I have time to put the brakes on my brain. Hadley is *not* my girl and can never be. Even if all of this works out, I'm never going to be enough for Hadley Crawford.

Hadley isn't necessarily dressed for work in a distillery. She's wearing jeans of the painted-on variety and a plaid shirt tied at the waist. All that would be a little Daisy Duke, perhaps, but still reasonable for a place as potentially dirty as Eddie's.

It's the shoes that push Hadley out of reasonable territory.

It's always the shoes with Hadley. I don't think I've ever seen her in town without some kind of sky-high heel on her feet. She's not particularly short, but in heels she gains a few inches, to be sure. When I was here in Mint Springs for the summers, I'd see her barefoot at the river, her painted toes always matching whichever bikini she'd decided to wear. And I've kissed her when she wasn't wearing shoes, after she'd kicked them off in the hayloft and had to rise up on the tips of her toes to be able to reach my lips.

If there's one thing I should not think about while looking at Hadley, it's her lips. Their pillow softness and the way they used to taste a bit like strawberries haunts me to this day. There has never been another set of lips I've kissed that have stuck with me the way Hadley's do. Sometimes, even with another woman, my brain will telegraph a memory of kissing her and then I'm done for the day. Sorry, folks, even if those memories have been exaggerated to epic proportions, there's no one who compares with Hadley.

"Right?" Eddie asks, and I suddenly realize the question's been directed at me.

I can't even pretend to have an idea what he's been talking about, so I just shrug. Luckily, Eddie's already pointing out something else to Hadley, so I look less like a fool. As she turns away and denies me the chance to look at her mouth one more time, Eddie catches my eye.

"Watch yourself, Cooper," he whispers. "That right there's dynamite you've got no business messing with." The look he gives me is supposed to let me know he's joking, but his words cut right to the heart of the matter. I'm doing my best to keep Hadley at arm's length.

"I know."

"Your shirt says otherwise." Eddie taps me on the chest. "Let's go teach your girl all about moonshine." He's sauntering off before I can argue, his arm linked with Hadley's.

14

Hadley

My initial assessment of Eddie's distillery, upon arrival? Not impressed. There's not even a sign out front to let you know there's anything going on inside this warehouse. What kind of a business doesn't bother hanging a sign? An unsuccessful one, that's what kind. The inside isn't much better. It's cluttered and crowded with things you wouldn't want customers to see. I'm already mentally cussing Cooper for wasting my afternoon before I've even met this Eddie person he keeps raving about.

But after a few minutes, I'm seeing potential.

Eddie's a bit gruff at the beginning, but cute as a button. He'd obviously not love me saying that in front of Cooper, but there's no denying how adorable this little gray-haired man is in his overalls. And when an occasional grin breaks out through all that unruly beard? I want to put him in my pocket and take him home.

Eddie knows his stuff, too, even if the place is a mess. He and Cooper take me back to the part of the warehouse where they make the liquor, and after a quick explanation of the process—and a warning to watch my step—I end up being impressed with Eddie's ability to explain even the most complicated parts. By the time we sit down to taste some of the finished product, I think I could probably make my own moonshine. Well, I could maybe get close.

The makeshift bar isn't the most comfortable place to sit —another minus for Eddie's—but Cooper pulls out a stool for me and tries to make me as comfortable as possible. And that's another thing about this afternoon at Eddie's—Cooper's being so...nice. Unusually nice, with none of his slight digs at me or hidden barbs. I start to relax around him a little, feel comfortable enough to joke with him a bit.

"This one here's one I hate to make, but people keep asking for it, so..." Eddie frowns as he pours me a taste.

"If people like it, then why do you not like to make it?" I pick up my little plastic thimble and smell the clear liquid inside it, nearly burning my nose hairs off. "Good Lord, is that supposed to be cinnamon?"

"It sure is. Taste it. You'll hate it." Eddie motions for me to take a sip.

"Should I shoot it?" I give it another sniff.

"No need to do that," Eddie says. "Save yourself for better options. Take a little sip and tell me what you think." He waits patiently while I ease the glass to my lips.

I swallow a tiny bit, letting it roll around in my mouth. "It isn't terrible, but I can't see myself drinking much of this." The cinnamon flavor overwhelms anything else, and by now I've tasted enough of Eddie's product to know it doesn't need to be covered up with flavorings.

"I take it you weren't a sorority girl." Eddie fishes around behind the bar, missing the slight frown I feel on my face at the mention of sororities. "It's supposed to taste like that cinnamon whiskey everyone drinks. I tried to make it less...

offensive, but people are used to the heavy cinnamon taste. They want it like a red hot candy. No subtlety." He scowls again. "But that's what happens when you make things to market." He looks accusingly at Cooper.

"I never said make it taste a certain way." Cooper acts aggrieved. "I just told you what people were coming in here asking for. I didn't force you to make it." He gives me a look like *can you get a load of this guy?* as he slides another tiny cup in front of me. "This one you'll like."

"Have some water first." Eddie hands me a bottle.

"Can I ask why you're using plastic for all of this?" I take a swig from the bottle and then reach for my new cup.

"Because Eddie hates to wash dishes." Cooper's smile is the one I remember from high school summers, the one he would wear when one of his brothers was caught in an embarrassing situation.

"Like you love it!" Eddie protests. "I haven't got all of this part figured out yet."

"Are you thinking about putting a sign out front? If you want people to come in for tours and tastings, you're going to need a sign. How long have you been here, anyway?"

Cooper's barely stifled laugh has Eddie fuming. "Not that long. And, yes, I'm going to get a sign. I just haven't gotten around to it."

I take a tentative sip of my new drink. "This is great. So smooth."

That seems to placate Eddie a bit. "That's what I mean. The good stuff is still the good stuff, but people always want to drink a candy bar or something stupid like that."

"Unfortunately, they're the customers, Eddie Mack. I keep telling you they'll come to love the better booze, but we need to get them in the door first." Cooper looks to me for confirmation. "If Hadley'd been walking down the street, she wouldn't have known this moonshine was in here waiting for her."

"That's true. I would never have known about this place if Cooper hadn't told me." I try not to be *too* deferential to Cooper. No need to make him think I'm going to agree with everything he says.

"And what did you think when you first came in?" Cooper asks me, refilling my minuscule glass.

"When I came in?" I down the thimble of alcohol to help me keep my initial thoughts to myself. While the interior was distracting, I'd actually been thinking about how handsome Cooper looked. He'd been leaned against the bar, the sunlight from the row of windows high above us glinting off his hair. I'd had trouble breathing for a second there after I'd pushed open that heavy glass door. That's not what Cooper's asking, though, and I'd rather crawl over broken glass than tell him any of that. "It was a little...distracting." There. Not a lie but not entirely the truth.

Cooper looks knowingly at Eddie. "See? Another pair of eyes helps. Explain that for us." He leans back a bit against the bar.

"Well..." I start, knowing Eddie's going to hate everything I say. "It's a little cluttered. And some of this stuff should probably be in the back, if this is going to be the first thing the customers see."

Cooper looks ready to high-five me. Eddie, on the other hand, is probably considering ways to kill me in my sleep.

"I'm getting around to all of this," Eddie says as he waves his arm around the room. "I care about the moonshine. All the rest is fluff."

"Fluff that sells the moonshine, Eddie." Cooper finishes his tiny sample and reaches out to touch my arm. The heat of his hand startles me, and I have to force myself not to pull away. His fingers singe my skin. "Hadley and I'll be able to tell you all about it after we do a few distillery tours."

"Distillery tours?" My mouth hangs open. "I thought *this* was the distillery tour."

"This is a start, but we'll need to see how successful ones operate. Luckily, there are plenty in driving distance." Cooper gives me a wink.

"How many of these tours are we talking about?" I picture an endless stream of long car rides and touristy experiences, all at the mercy of Cooper Allen. Absolutely not. No thank you.

"Not sure yet. We can talk about which ones we really want to see. We could do the entire Whiskey Trail. It'd be fun." Cooper bounces a little, his smile a mile wide.

"Fun?" This does not sound like fun to me. Having to look at Cooper for hours, trying to remember to hate him, knowing we're only spending time together as a means to an end, sounds awful.

"Looking forward to your report." Eddie folds his arms across his chest. "Sure you two will have a fabulous time." Then he gives me the grin I'd found so endearing before. It doesn't have the same effect now. "More shine?"

I put my thimble forward and let him fill it. I'm going to need more than moonshine to get through this.

15

Hadley

"I don't know, sounds fun to me, babe." Ryan takes another bite of his club sandwich and shrugs. He has no idea what he's talking about. Of course, that's because I haven't told him anything about Cooper Allen.

"Maybe," I hedge. "I just think it'll take up so much time —time I could be spending with you." I hope that comes out coy instead of desperate. I don't want to scare Ryan off this early in the game.

Of course, bringing him to Ham & Eggs during the lunch rush was probably not the best way to keep Ryan from running. Currently we're the entertainment for all of Mint Springs as they munch on their fries and finish their lemonade. People are lingering, and I don't think it's because of the soup of the day. Necks have been craning since we sat down, especially since Debbie put us at a table in the middle of the room.

"Aw, that's sweet, babe, but I'm sure we'll still have plenty of time together. A few distillery visits won't change that."

Ryan winks. I'm not entirely sold on the idea of him calling me 'babe,' but I let that go for now.

"How's everything over here?" Debbie swoops in to refill our iced teas. "How's your sandwich?" She turns toward Ryan and flutters her eyelashes. Debbie might be older, but she's still got her tricks.

"The sandwich is great, thanks." Ryan gives Debbie a smile, showing off all those perfect white teeth. "My compliments to the chef." He motions back toward the window where Henry's manning the grill. He's the only person in this diner not currently watching Ryan and Debbie like it's *Days of Our Lives*.

"I'll let the guys know you enjoyed it. Are you visiting? I thought I knew just about everybody in Mint Springs." Debbie gives me a pointed look. Only in this town would people call you to task for your manners for not introducing your lunch date to the waitress.

"Debbie, this is Ryan. Ryan, this is Debbie, the queen of Ham & Eggs."

"Well, I'm hardly the queen," Debbie demurs. "I can't compete with the likes of Hadley here." She gives me a quick glance, most likely finding fault with the length of my skirt.

Ryan smiles. He doesn't know his next move is supposed to be to compliment Debbie even if it means taking a little of my shine. Debbie waits patiently, but Ryan doesn't know all these rules, so he goes back to eating his sandwich, oblivious to Debbie's raised eyebrow and startled expression.

"Now, Debbie, you know you're always the prettiest girl in this room." It doesn't mean the same coming from me, and Debbie doesn't hide it. She purses her lips and takes her pitcher of tea elsewhere.

"Tell me about this Cooper guy," Ryan says through a mouth full of sandwich.

Immediately I sit up a little bit straighter. "What?" I try to concentrate on cutting the smallest possible bite of my Hot Brown.

"Cooper. He's your partner, right?" Ryan takes a sip of his tea, completely unaware of how sweaty my palms are becoming.

"There's not much to tell, really," I lie. "He used to come here in the summers to stay with his grandfather, so he's not local, exactly, but I've known him for a while." I leave out the part about having kissed him a million times, and don't mention how Cooper carved our initials into the barn wall because we were going to last forever.

"And you two got paired up in this online class? That's lucky." He puts another bite of turkey and toasted bread into his mouth.

"Lucky?" That's the last thing I'd call it.

"Sure. You already know each other, and he's actually close by. He lives here now, right?" Ryan nods his blond head at one of the Mathis twins as she passes by. Once she's behind him she turns around and mouths *oh my*, letting me know exactly how she feels about Ryan's undeniable handsomeness. I try and ignore her as I focus on a way to talk about Cooper without giving too much away.

"He does. His brother's married to Lily."

Ryan stares at me blankly.

"You remember Lily, right?"

Ryan's lips quirk up. "Wait, your friend, right?"

"My *best* friend, Ryan. She has the design business, used to live with me when she moved back from Chicago, disgustingly in love with her husband? Any of this ringing a bell?"

"Yes, yes. I remember. Sorry, babe. I guess her name slipped my mind." He shrugs. "So, Cooper's your friend-in-law or something like that."

"Something like that." *Friend-in-law?* A thousand other ways to describe Cooper jump into my head. *The bane of my existence. A class A jerk. The one that got away. The love of my life.* Those last two surprise even me.

"I can't wait to meet him." Ryan's distractedly fishing around in his pocket. "Um, sorry. I should really take this." He holds up his phone. "Work stuff. Be right back." He stands and turns toward the front door, but then takes a step toward me and gives me an awkward kiss on the top of my head. Several murmurs let me know the entire diner saw that move.

As Ryan walks out the door of Ham & Eggs, I focus on the good things. He's tall and handsome. Normally a better conversationalist. He has a good job and so far isn't a serial killer. He has a fantastic butt—one that I can admire as he walks out onto the sidewalk at the exact same moment Cooper Allen walks in.

16

Cooper

Hadley's smiling face is the first thing I see once my eyes adjust from the sunshine outside. She's beaming, and I automatically smile right back at her, a full-on grin that splits my face before I can control myself. I've always been a sucker for Hadley's smile. It's second only to her laugh—this full, throaty thing that makes my head fuzzy. It is impossible for me to think when Hadley's really laughing. But it's been a while since I've gotten to hear a genuine Hadley belly laugh —even longer since I've been gifted with a real smile—so seeing her today makes me almost giddy.

And then that giant smile slides right off her face. In its place is the hard, thin line I would have thought she could never make with those lips of hers. But she can make it, alright. It's the main way I see her looking at me lately. That earlier grin wasn't for me.

She's sitting dead in the center of Ham & Eggs, and it looks like she isn't here alone. All eyes in the diner now shift from Hadley and her lunch to me frozen in the doorway. I shake off any of the disappointment at Hadley's reaction to me and saunter in like I own the place. I make a beeline for her and pull out an empty chair, making myself at home at Hadley's table.

"You *cannot* sit there," Hadley hisses at me.

"Obviously I can. Don't worry, Hadley, I'll sit here with you. Hate to see anyone eating alone." I put my hands behind my head and stretch out my legs for effect.

"I'm not alone." She gestures to the half-eaten sandwich and plate of fries in front of me.

"You here with Lily?" I ask as I reach for one of those fries, more than prepared to pop one in my mouth. Truth be told, I know Hadley isn't here with Lily, because I've volunteered to do the lunch run in order to escape Lily and my brother and their over-the-top need to show the world how much they love each other. I'd tell them to get a room, but they've got one, and most of the time I'm the extra person standing in it.

Hadley slaps my hand away from the plate. "I am not here with Lily, and even if I was you can't just help yourself to someone else's lunch." She looks at me like I'm some kind of Neanderthal.

"Lily wouldn't mind sharing with me." I try again to snag a French fry and am met with another Hadley block.

"I told you. I'm not here with Lily. You need to get your butt out of that seat right now." Hadley's eyes flash fire and there's no way I'm moving now. I might love Hadley laughing, but angry Hadley does something to me too, and I'm not about to give that up willingly.

"Leave you alone for a minute and some other guy moves in to take my place."

I look up into the face of a stranger. He's smiling, not at all aware that there's a significant part of me more than willing to take his place here with Hadley. An uncomfortable bubble of jealousy has me clearing my throat as I stand.

"Sorry. I was keeping Hadley company." I extend my hand. "I'm Cooper. I don't think we've met."

"Ryan," he says as we shake. "Hadley and I were just talking about you, weren't we, babe?"

I notice the barely-there wince from Hadley. She's not the kind to appreciate being anyone's "babe." It's too brusque, too casual, not a term of endearment at all. Not for Hadley.

"You were?" I look at Hadley, and she nearly growls at me. "All good things I hope." I doubt Hadley's got many good things to say about me, but her friend hasn't punched me in the face yet, so either she's been playing nice, or he isn't the kind of guy to hit someone without giving them fair warning.

"We were talking about our project. About us being partners." Hadley gives me an extremely fake smile.

"I was saying she's lucky to be matched up with someone she already knows." Ryan's still standing, the two of us milling about in the aisle, ostensibly blocking Debbie from getting past with the lunch orders, but she's only using that as an excuse to stand too close to us. All eyes are on our table now, the customers of Ham & Eggs hanging on every word that comes out of our mouths.

"I don't know about that," I counter. "I can be difficult to work with."

"So can Hadley, I imagine," Ryan laughs. "She's pretty obstinate when she wants to be."

Hadley doesn't smile at this like it's some kind of inside joke. Instead, her brow furrows, and her mouth goes back to its flat line from before. It's not the face she should be making on a date, and I consider saying something that will make her laugh, even if it's at my expense. That's not my job right now, though. Right now she's here with another man. With Ryan.

"I'll let you two get back to your lunch. Sorry to interrupt." I start to back away from Hadley and her date.

"Thanks for keeping my girl company," Ryan says as he reclaims his seat. "Wouldn't want her to get lonely."

His declaration that Hadley's *his girl* surprises her more than it does me. The look on her face keeps me from correcting him, letting it slip that Hadley's never going to be anyone's girl but mine, not really. I can't blurt that out here in the diner anyway, can't blurt that out anywhere to anyone. It's hard to keep it to myself on an ordinary day, but on a day when I find Hadley on a date with a guy who looks like a viable contender, it's damn near impossible.

I keep my fists at my sides as I grunt out my goodbyes and escape to the counter, where my pick-up order's growing colder by the minute.

"What you gonna do about that, you figure?" Debbie asks as she rings me up.

"Nothing to do about that, Debbie. Looks like Hadley's got herself a boyfriend. Not my business one way or the other." I stuff the change she gives me into the tip jar.

"You keep telling yourself that, Cooper." Debbie sighs. "That girl wasn't going to wait forever, but that boy's not perfect."

"Nobody asked her to wait, Debbie." I carry the paper bag out to my truck and drive away from Hadley Crawford and the thing I've been hoping she'd find.

I just hadn't counted on it hurting this much.

17

Hadley

"You didn't have to drive; we could have taken my car."

"Is that a subtle dig at this fine automobile, Hadley? Because I will not have you disrespecting this truck." Cooper smiles at me. "That's sarcasm, in case you missed it."

"Oh, I got it." I try to control my eye rolling. We're only thirty minutes into this trip, and already we're having to clearly state our intentions. We're like an old married couple, or maybe one about to divorce.

"I'm driving because I can hold my liquor better than you can." Cooper keeps his eyes on the road, steering with both hands.

"You know that's not true." Not that I want to get into a contest about who is the bigger drinker—I think my mother and grandmother would strongly discourage that—but I don't like for Cooper to be able to best me at anything.

"Okay, you can hold your own, I'll give you that. But you're smaller than me. That alone makes it easier for me to drink more than you."

"We're tasting, Cooper, not tying one on." I stare at his

profile. He's got the same nose as his brother Chance, the kind you find on movie stars and models. The kind that's wasted on a man, even if he is as pretty as Cooper. He'd hate for me to use that word to describe him—most men don't want to be pretty—but Cooper's got a little bit of that pretty boy aura about him, from his looks to his luck. Not sure what happened to make that second one run out, but he isn't suffering in the first area. Not at all.

"You're right. Neither one of us is driving home today with anything close to a buzz. No need to push it. I think we can get plenty of information without drinking the place dry." He smiles again. "Unless you want to take advantage and have me be your designated driver."

"No, thank you." I don't even have to think about that. Relying on Cooper is something I try not to do if I can help it. It's part of the reason this project is still making me nervous. "Did you get a chance to read the article I sent you?"

"Article?" Cooper is a terrible liar. He's got the world's most obvious tell when he bends the truth even a little bit. It's how I can always beat him in poker although he's never managed to figure it out. From this angle I have no problem seeing his right eye twitch just a fraction.

"The one about the family that reopened their distillery with the great-great grandfather's recipe? I emailed it to you two days ago." I glare even though Cooper isn't going to see it.

"Huh. I don't think I saw it." Another twitch. "Why don't you tell me about it?"

This isn't the first time Cooper's shirked his responsibility. Sure, the professor didn't assign this article, but for our project to be a success, we need to do enough research for this to be automatic. Cooper may know more about the process of distilling than I do, but I'm burning my retinas with article after article and book after book to catch up. The least he could do is read some of the things I send him.

"Do you have a copy with you?" He still doesn't turn to look at me. "Maybe you could read it to me. Then we'd be on the same page."

I groan like a middle school girl. Cooper really brings out the best in me. "I brought the magazine with me." I pull it out of my bag. It's the Whiskey Trail edition of a glossy regional magazine. Several of the distilleries featured in the articles I've read seem like exactly what Cooper's looking to do. I flip to the article I want and have to stifle a sigh of longing.

There's the most gorgeous photo of this family on the first page—all of them posed in front of their fabulous house. I know it probably isn't reality, but it's the kind of family I dream of having one day. Children of my own with plenty of cousins to play with nearby. Maybe this family spends Thanksgiving arguing over the dinner table, but from this photo you'd never guess. They've got an easy way about them, crisp shirts on the men and flowing dresses on the ladies in front of the impossible green and purple of the wisteria in the background.

"What?" Cooper asks, finally giving me a glance.

"Nothing. I just love this photo. I'd show it to you, but you're supposed to be driving." I motion toward the windshield, and Cooper goes back to facing front.

"Tell me about it." Cooper's hand comes out to turn down the radio, leaving it as only a hum in the background. "What made you sigh like that?"

"Did I do that out loud?" My cheeks heat with a tinge of mortification.

"You did," Cooper confirms, but he isn't teasing me.

I wait for the sarcasm I'm sure is about to follow but only get another encouraging smile. After a few beats I give in.

"It's hard to explain, really. It's a beautiful picture. They've got this lovely house, obviously, and they're all dressed perfectly. But it's more than the way it looks; it's the way it feels. Like they actually like each other and get along. Like they'd choose to spend time together even if they weren't family. It's aspirational, I guess." I've said too much, I think. Given Cooper too much ammunition. I brace myself for at least a bit of ridicule.

"Why's that aspirational?" Cooper's question sounds genuine.

"Well, that's what I'd like to find some day." Again, that's not information I should give Cooper Allen, of all people.

"You don't find that, Hadley—you make it."

I startle a bit. My head spins in Cooper's direction. He's still focused on the road, his fingers drumming on the steering wheel.

"Maybe you'll be able to make something like that with Ryan." His jaw ticks. "If that's what you want, I'm sure you'll be able to make it happen."

I blink, trying to focus on the words printed out in front of me. "I hope so," I say even though that's not really what I mean. Right now I'm not hoping for a family photo like this with Ryan. I'm trying to keep myself from imagining Cooper there next to me, holding my hand. Because that easy feeling? It's happening right now, here in this beat-up old truck. It's happening with Cooper as we drive toward an entire day together.

I clear my throat and start to read.

18

Cooper

"No, you did not!" Hadley tips her head back and laughs. It's loud enough that other people turn to look at us. I'm not even self-conscious about having people stare; right now the only thing I care about is keeping Hadley laughing.

"I told you I did. If I hadn't left the car in drive, no one would have ever found out, but I was barely fifteen, so I wasn't completely clear on all the steps, you know." I take another sip of the whiskey in front of me. This trip's been a success in more ways than one. We've gotten plenty of information for the business plan, and I've had a terrific time with Hadley.

"And it rolled into the tomato patch?"

I nod and Hadley howls.

"Rolled all the way in. Not even to the edge or anything. Like dead through it, almost to the other side." I imitate the truck with my hand. "Right over everything."

"I can actually picture your grandpa's face. Is that bad? I shouldn't be laughing at that, but good Lord, Cooper, I would have paid good money to see how that worked out in the morning." Hadley wipes away tears.

"There was a fair amount of yelling." I'm laughing too, telling this ridiculous story to Hadley. "And then a full day of Chance and I trying to stake anything we could to try and save those plants. It wasn't particularly successful, as you can probably imagine."

"And Sadie and Mae? What did your aunts say?"

"They didn't say much, just wouldn't let us have any dessert for what felt like forever. Chance and I would have to watch Charlie and Cade eat theirs, and they'd drag it out, you know? Make us all sit at the table while they took these tiny bites of pie. Torture."

"But so deserved, Cooper, and I cannot think of a worse punishment for adolescent boys than to deny them dessert." Hadley takes another sip of her drink and moans. "This one's my favorite, I think."

I swallow hard. I cannot take much more of Hadley's moans. "You've said that about every one we've tasted."

"Have I?" Hadley lifts her glass and considers the amber liquid inside it, then gives me a grin. "I probably have."

"Should we get going here in a minute?" I don't want to leave yet, but at least I've got an hour in the car with Hadley to look forward to. Maybe I can get her to read to me again, let her voice wash over me the way it did on the drive down here.

I'd felt bad at first about ignoring the article she sent. Not that I was ignoring it, really—more like putting off the inevitable misery of trying to read it and then not remembering a word. I know it was probably supposed to be some fluff article, but it'd trip me up just the same, give me the same headache and wasted afternoon with nothing to show for it that *all* books give me.

But having Hadley read to me made me congratulate myself on a choice well-made. Now, I've heard all about the Baldwin's family distillery and gotten another piece of the Hadley puzzle. I'd had to slow my heart when she didn't immediately jump on the idea of Ryan as the start of her dream family. I'd been ready to at least not give her any snark about it if she told me that was how she was feeling. For her to let it go without comment gave me more hope than I should let myself have, especially if I want Hadley to end up with someone who's worthy of her.

In this moment, I'm feeling worthy of her, though. Making her laugh, watching her enjoy herself. If this was all it took—if this was all she needed—I'd gladly throw Ryan off the closest bridge and get to work making Hadley happy. That's not all she needs, though, and I'd be pretending if I said I could give her more than that.

"Could we stay a little longer?" Hadley asks, those big blue eyes having their way with me. "We could have dinner. My treat. We should check out the restaurant anyway, right? That's research, Cooper." She gives me a pleading look. "Unless you have something you need to get back to…"

All I've got waiting for me at home is watching Chance and Lily make eyes at each other. There's nothing more pressing right now than giving Hadley what she wants while I have the opportunity to do it.

"You're buying?" I pretend to think about it. "I could probably be talked into that."

"You need me to convince you? Come on, Cooper. That restaurant is your *competition*. We have to eat there." Hadley makes a serious face. "And I'm starving."

"Alright, I guess." I get up off my bar stool. Hadley and I started out doing the tasting a few hours ago and have been hogging these spots ever since. It's probably the least we can do to have dinner in their restaurant. I extend my hand and, to my surprise, Hadley takes it. It's a good thing, too, because she teeters a little bit. Her usual crazy shoes don't help the situation.

"Oh, oops." Hadley leans up against me, steading herself. I get a whiff of her perfume as she ends up entirely too close to me. It's the same one she used to wear, the one I know very well because my face has been tucked in the crook of her neck before. My entire body reacts to that familiar scent, and I find myself sliding an arm around Hadley's waist instead of pulling away.

"Let's get some food in you." I guide her past the other tourists in the tasting room and out toward the restaurant. This distillery isn't supposed to be one of the fancy ones, but the little white lights twinkling around the front porch of the place make it seem special. Hadley and I've already taken a million photos of the buildings, taking note of the way things are decorated. We've made note of the equipment we were able to see and guesses about what we couldn't.

"Oh, take a photo of me at the top of the stairs," Hadley orders. "This entrance is so pretty."

I deposit Hadley at the top of the stairs, letting her go reluctantly. She poses, and I take multiple photos with my phone, pretending to be interested in the entrance to the restaurant, but really only focusing on Hadley.

Once we're seated, Hadley can't get over the menu, *ohhing* and *ahhing* over the choices. I find myself smiling in spite of myself, listening to her decide what to order.

"Maybe the salmon?" She hesitates. "I'm always disappointed. They overcook it. When you have your restaurant, make sure the chef knows how to properly cook salmon. That's as a favor to me, okay?"

"I'll do my best."

Hadley beams at me, and I swear everything that's happened before melts away. It's just me and Hadley, enjoying time together. I know it's all pretend and tomorrow we'll probably be back to hating each other, but I'm going to suspend disbelief for as long as I can.

Dinner means Hadley moaning again, and there's no way to put a stop to it. She loves everything, and I wonder if this is what life with Hadley would be like. I'm used to the more abrasive side, not this enthusiastic person sitting across from me enjoying the hell out of her scallops.

"You have got to taste this," Hadley says around a mouthful of risotto. "I have died and gone to heaven."

Our server smiles at Hadley as he drops her third cocktail at the table.

"Ohhh," Hadley says as she reaches for the glass. Normally I'd make some crack about her being lucky to have such a responsible designated driver, but I bite my tongue. It's nice to have Hadley relaxed. This is how I remember her, even if she might not remember this tomorrow. I keep sipping on my water, focusing on Hadley and her love of everything in this restaurant.

"This is delicious," Hadley announces. "Which one is this?" She reaches for the drink menu and scans the card. "The one with the mint in it? Do you see mint in there?" She thrusts the glass at me. "Here taste it."

I do as I'm told, even if I'm currently relegated to water.

"It's good," I confirm even if I'd probably prefer my whiskey straight.

"We're going to have specialty cocktails too, right?" She takes another sip. "We have to, don't you think?"

"What's this 'we' business?" I cock an eyebrow at Hadley. "You a customer, or are you thinking about investing?"

"Investing?" Hadley snorts. "I'm in on the ground floor, Cooper. Just try and get rid of me. And you owe me, don't forget about that."

I smile, even if I can already feel the punch to the gut Hadley's words are giving me. I've tried to get rid of her, over and over again. I know she's not serious, but the fact that I'd like her to be shows how weak I am when I want something.

"I love that this place has a story. The whole thing about the way the family started making whiskey and all the interesting stuff about the land it's built on. We need to come up with something like that for our business plan. Something that humanizes things, you know?" Hadley taps a finger to her chin. "Think on that, will you, genius?"

"We both know who the genius here is. I'm going to leave that to you." I'm not even joking. I'm crazy about Hadley's brain. It doesn't hurt it's housed inside the prettiest package I've ever seen.

When dinner's over, we fight for the check, our hands connecting repeatedly as we squabble.

"But it was my idea," Hadley nearly wails. "It's supposed to be my treat." She looks close to crying, but I recognize crocodile tears when I see them.

"A gentleman never lets a lady pay, Hadley." I hand my credit card to the server with a flourish. The price of dinner is a bargain for having had Hadley's company all day.

I see Hadley hold in her scoff at my gentleman claim. "But I ordered so much stuff. I would never have done that if I had thought you were going to pay, Cooper."

It burns that she's thinking about money right now, specifically my lack of it.

"I do alright, Hadley." I ignore the twinge of pity I think I see on her face. "Let me pay for this."

She's quiet on the car ride back home. We've got plenty

of time, but we spend most of it in silence, just the sound of the radio filling the cab. Hadley rolls down the window and lets the wind blow her hair around a little. I keep sneaking glances at her, looking at the relaxed way she leans against the headrest, looking out at the night as we drive along. She's had enough to drink to keep her soft, even though I'd never underestimate the way Hadley can switch back to hard edges if she wants. Occasionally she catches me looking at her, but more often than not when I try to sneak a look at her, she's already looking right back.

I pull up in front of her apartment, sad for the night to end. I've gotten used to fighting with Hadley, verbally sparring at every opportunity. Today there's been hardly any of that, and I'm going to be disappointed to go back to it. We'll have to eventually. Being friends with her is too dangerous.

"I guess that's it, then." Hadley reaches for the door handle. "I had a nice time, Cooper." Her admission is guarded, and I don't blame her. This is where I should try to deny I've enjoyed it, try to get a barb or two in. She braces for it, her shoulders tensing, and that familiar set of her mouth coming back in place of her smile.

But I don't do what I should; instead I do what I want, for once. "I had a good time, too. Let me walk you up." I'm sure there's no real safety concern here in the parking lot of Hadley's building, but I use chivalry as an excuse for five more minutes with her like this.

Hadley doesn't fight me, although she doesn't wait for me to come around to open her door. *It's not a date,* I remind myself, even though it's the best time I've had in a while, date or no date. We meet in front of the truck, entirely too close as I walk her to her door. Once we get there, Hadley turns. I'm ready to say my goodbyes when those eyes catch mine.

The air grows thick between us, her lips in easy striking distance of mine. I could close the distance between us, wrap my arms around her and kiss her like I've wanted to right here, right now, consequences be damned. Hadley's looking at me like she'd be more than amenable to kissing. Her gaze moves between my eyes and my lips, telegraphing what she wants. Her lips part, inviting me to move closer and taste her. I'm ready to lean in when another car comes rolling into the parking lot, breaking the spell. I pull away from her.

"I'll text you about getting together to share notes," I call out as I back away from her, already halfway to the truck. Hadley stands like a statue in front of the door. "Go ahead and go in, Hadley," I coax, needing her to be safely tucked in her apartment before I can get back in the truck.

"Cooper..." Her face clouds, but she turns toward the door and lets herself in, obviously reconsidering whatever she was about to say.

I sit in the truck for at least five minutes, letting my heart stop trying to beat its way out of my chest. Forget about trying to make her hate me, I nearly proved exactly how I feel about Hadley right here on her front porch. *Get it together, Cooper.* There's too much on the line for me to muddy things up with Hadley, and I've spent too much time denying myself to ruin it all for her now.

You're not what she wants, I chant to myself all the way home.

19

Hadley

Was he going to kiss me? Cooper Allen was *definitely* going to kiss me. The worst part was, I was going to let him. I was going to *more than* let him, I was *hoping* he would. If my neighbor hadn't chosen to come home at that exact moment, Cooper and I would have been in a lip lock for the ages. My mouth tingles thinking about the way he'd looked at me.

Which is not what I should be thinking about as I detail the latest on my relationship with Ryan to my older sister.

"He sounds great, Hadley. It was time for you to seek out a little new blood." Mindy's voice crackles on the other end of the line. I can hear my nephew in the background still chattering away, despite Mindy's attempt to drive him around until he falls asleep.

"You make me sound like a vampire."

"If you were a vampire, I wouldn't have to spend so much time trying to convince you to settle down. Vampires live forever, and they don't age." Mindy's basically yelling.

"Am I on speaker? How can Caleb fall asleep with you

talking so loudly?" I'm not sure Mindy thought through calling me during the naptime drive.

"I can't be expected to spend all day with no adult contact, can I?" Caleb's only two, but Mindy's marriage is already on the rocks. Her prince charming leaves for work early and comes home late. Mindy thought she'd hit the jackpot when she married Devin, but it turns out the life she thought she'd love isn't all it's cracked up to be.

"No, but... Why don't you let Caleb fall asleep and then call me back?"

"Why don't you stop holding out on me and get to the good stuff? What kind of pocket rocket are we dealing with here?"

"I beg your pardon? *Pocket rocket*?" My sister has lost her mind.

"I can't exactly use the words I want to right now, Hadley. His tally whacker. His pecker. His cock-a-doodle-doo. Just tell me if we're working with regulation size." Mindy waits as the silence grows between us. Only Caleb's babbling fills the space. "Bigger?" Mindy demands. "Or... Oh, no, Hadley. Smaller? A chicken little? Oh, honey."

"No, I mean..." I do not want to talk about Ryan's *pocket rocket* with my sister, especially since I don't have any first-hand knowledge of what he might be keeping in his pants. "I don't actually know."

"You don't know?" Mindy screeches, causing my nephew to voice his displeasure with a loud burst of crying. "It's been weeks! How can you not know?"

"We're taking it slow," I tell her. That's only half the truth. Ryan had originally liked my idea to draw things out, but he won't find any of that charming for long. Normally I'm not big on waiting; I'm a firm believer in try before you buy. But in this instance I'm having an unusual issue.

Cooper.

Specifically, Cooper and the time we've been spending together.

"Well, you'd better try to lock that down, little sister. A man like that probably has a line out the door." Caleb's volume increases and Mindy shushes him. "I have to let you go; I can't drive with the baby screaming like this. You think about what I said, though. No use in waiting if you think he's a keeper, Hadley."

And she hangs up on me.

Mindy's right. Men like Ryan don't wait around forever. And he's interested and available—two things Cooper Allen is not, even if he were a reasonable candidate. Still, the other night with Cooper, there were some real sparks. I'm sure of it.

And it hadn't been a date. Not technically. But it had started to feel like one, although maybe that was the whiskey talking. Cooper being civil shouldn't have me falling all over him. He needs me to pass this class and be able to dazzle his brothers with his distillery plan. Of course he's going to be nice; if he isn't, he stands to lose the best project partner he could ever hope to find—not that we have a choice.

I open up my laptop and write Cooper an email. I'm all business. It might as well be on letterhead with all the formalities I'm throwing at him. We need to meet to go over our information so far, but I want to be sure any getting together is as sexy as granny panties. Which is to say, not very. Unless you're my grandmother, who most likely still has something incredibly racy on under her bedazzled jeans.

I hit send and start to shut the computer when Cooper's response pops up. He can't have even read my message with a response time like that. I get ready to cuss Cooper Allen and his lazy, good-for-nothing ass. I click, already mentally composing my sassy answers to any questions he might dare to ask. But it isn't a message that starts to load on my computer screen.

It's a photo.

A photo of Cooper and me together, smiling, sitting shoulder to shoulder. He'd asked our waiter to take it under the guise of looking less like a bunch of trade-secret-stealing thieves and more like a couple. It had been our running joke all day—that we were basically secret agents out to make off with whatever whiskey knowledge we could get. Not that anyone at that distillery cared or probably would give a flying flip about us considering a column still instead of a pot still based on their tour.

And Cooper and I must be exceptional actors, because we do look like a couple. We're looking at the camera, heads tilted slightly together, big smiles on our faces. Cooper's arm is around me, and I'm surprised you can't see the goose-bumps that had exploded all over my body when his hand made contact with my back. I can feel them now, looking at this photo. What's worse is I want to feel them again, have Cooper's arm draped around my shoulders, his fingers barely grazing my shoulder blades. We don't look like we're faking anything, and I know for a fact I'm not. I don't have to pretend to have feelings for Cooper, because despite the past year of trying to hate him, I've still got that flutter in my belly, feelings close enough to the surface that this is exposing them to the light of day.

And once those things get a little sunshine, they're bound to grow.

20

Cooper

"I don't understand why we need to meet here, though. Your apartment worked great last time and at least Patty Cakes has coffee. This isn't exactly a quiet place to work." I set my stuff down on the table in the back of Hot House Flowers. It's probably someone's old cast-off kitchen table. There are deep scratches on the top, and it's got one wobbly leg that protests under the weight of my computer bag.

"I have a few clients today. I thought we could work in between, maybe?" Hadley's sweeter than she needs to be, which always raises my hackles a little bit. She's dressed for work, which means slightly lower heels than usual but the same painted-on jeans I'm going to have to try to ignore all day.

"You don't think it'll be distracting to try and go through our notes with all that other going on?" I wave a dismissive arm in the direction of the other Hot House ladies and their clients. It's only nine in the morning, but Saturdays appear to be busy days in the salon. Already most of the chairs are full of chatty women, all of them way too interested in why

I'm sitting here and not trying to be discreet about it. "What did you tell them we're doing?"

"I told them I'm helping you with your dating profile." Hadley gives me a little jazz hands. "We can try to figure out another day, I guess, but we need to maximize our time, Cooper. I don't want us to end up rushing at the last minute." She frowns.

"Fine." I give in, always defenseless against Hadley's pout. "But don't get mad at me if I get distracted. It's not exactly a library in here."

Hadley gives me a look I think I've seen on my mother before. "Try, Cooper. Focus."

Easier said than done. Hadley goes off to squirt a bunch of who knows what on some older lady's head, and I try to get my notes organized. Truthfully, I don't have much to do. I'm not big on writing things down. I've been using our photos to refresh my memory about our distillery visit. Most of my information's in my head, not down on paper or typed into a Word document. Looking at those photos has one obvious downside, though. They may be helping me to remember the placement of things or the lighting, but they're also keeping one thing in the forefront of my mind.

Hadley.

Her face is in nearly all the photos I took, and it's impossible for me to look at her and not remember our near kiss. I've got a constant reminder of how pretty she looked over dinner, just in case my brain has managed to forget. It hasn't, obviously, and right now it's reminding me again about the chance I had to touch Hadley the way I want to and all the reasons I absolutely cannot get myself in a situation like that again. Maybe working at Hot House Flowers is the safest idea for both of us.

I steal another glance at Hadley while she works. She's

smiling, laughing at something the tiny, gray-haired lady in the chair is saying. She tips her head back every so often, and I get the full expanse of her throat as her laughter fills the salon. There's no shortage of hilarious jokes coming out of this elfin lady's mouth, apparently, because Hadley's laughing like she's at a comedy show and this senior citizen's the headliner. I smile in spite of myself, forgetting to hide my interest in Hadley, enjoying the banter she's got going with her client and the homey feel of the salon.

That all comes to an abrupt end when Hadley's sister comes waltzing in the front door. She's juggling a cup of coffee and an oversized bag and gives me a death glare as soon as she sees me. I swallow hard. Mindy Crawford hates me. Although now that she's married, her last name must not be Crawford anymore. Not that this matters, because she's one hundred percent Crawford in ways that a name change can never erase—she's opinionated, sassy, and not at all afraid to tell me to fuck off. I can see she's considering the last one once the door shuts behind her.

"What in the hell is he doing here?" Mindy scowls at me and dumps her bag in one of the empty salon chairs.

"Good to see you again, Mindy." If I'd known she was going to be here I would have done more to convince Hadley we should meet somewhere else. Hell, if I'd known Mindy was anywhere near Mint Springs, I probably would have left town to ensure I didn't run into her.

Mindy acknowledges me with a loud *harrumph*. So much for manners. "Please tell me Cooper isn't here with you," she begs Hadley.

"He is, but it's not what you think—" Hadley starts to explain when Mindy cuts her off with a raised hand.

"I don't need to know the details; I just need to know he's going to be leaving in the next five minutes. I cannot be expected to do hair with him camped out in the break room."

"He's going to be here for a while, Mindy." Hadley keeps working on the head full of curlers in front of her.

"Please do not tell me you have gone and lost your mind and forgiven him. Not after what he did." Mindy doesn't lower her voice, and now every head in Hot House Flowers is looking in my direction.

"Cooper and I have a working relationship."

"I think we all know how Cooper *works*. No wonder you're messing things up with Ryan." Mindy lets out an exasperated sigh that's meant to keep all eyes on her, but I'm looking only at Hadley. She keeps her head down and her eyes on her work.

She's messing things up with Ryan? Now you've got my full attention, Mindy.

"Girls!" The reprimand is sharp and comes from the red-lipped mouth of Hadley's mother. "Is this the kind of ambiance we want in here? Mindy, get your station set up and leave Cooper alone. You're jeopardizing your Saturday shift acting like this." She turns back to her client but gives me a wink first.

Good Lord, I do not need all this time with the Crawford women. What was I thinking? Hot House Flowers on a Saturday is something I'll avoid in the future. In fact, I'll plan on avoiding Hot House Flowers entirely from now on.

"Okay, what've you got?" Hadley plops down in the seat next to me. "I've got fifteen minutes while Marjorie sits under the heat lamp." She leans over and I get a whiff of her, rendering my brain completely useless. Which is why when she reaches for my laptop, I'm not ready to block her.

She spins the thing around, and there, filling up the whole screen, is my favorite photo of Hadley from our day trip. She's posed in front of the distillery tour sign, one finger pointing in the same direction as the painted arrow. Her lips are stuck out in an exaggerated pout. We'd missed the first tour and had to wait around until the next one, extending our time at the distillery and our time together. I'd been annoyed at first, thinking if Hadley hadn't spent so much time checking out every single thing she saw on our way into the building we'd have been on time. Of course, if we had, I wouldn't have gotten to spend all day with her and I wouldn't have this photo to obsess over. It isn't meant to be seductive, but it's hotter than anything I've seen on the Internet *ever*. The way Hadley's looking at the camera and the way her body's angled has been keeping me up at night.

Hadley's eyes widen when she sees the screen. She blinks, wrinkling her forehead in confusion. "Cooper, why are you—"

"Good morning, ladies!"

For a second I think I'm saved, thanking my lucky stars for whoever's coming in the front door. But it's not the cavalry.

It's Ryan.

He's got one of those cardboard holders full of disposable coffee cups, and he does not look happy to see me sitting here with Hadley. The way he squares his shoulders and forces a smile tells me he wasn't factoring me into this coffee delivery.

"Anyone need a cup of coffee?" Ryan moves through the salon like he's been here before, handing out cups and flashing smiles. "And for you, Abilene, I got one of those fancy chocolate ones you like."

"Thank you, sugar." Hadley's mother takes the cup and smiles at Ryan. "So nice of you to think of us."

Ryan finishes handing out the drinks he has, finally

giving one to Hadley with a flourish. "And for you, a latte, extra hot." He makes sure to kiss her full on the mouth. "Would have gotten you something, Cooper, but I didn't realize you were going to be here. And I don't know your order the way I do Hadley's." He smiles over at her like the cat who ate the canary as he reaches out to shake my hand.

Hadley takes the cup and blows a little on the beverage through the hole in the plastic top. "Thank you." She takes a sip and pulls back, surprised.

Ryan doesn't seem to register that anything's wrong. He stands there smiling, like he's the king of the world, and I guess that's partly right, but I know exactly what's wrong with Hadley. He's forgotten something important about how Hadley Crawford likes her coffee.

"No cinnamon?" I ask, keeping my eyes focused on my computer screen, working to minimize all the photos I had pulled up.

Hadley ignores me, reaching for Ryan's hand. "Come meet Mindy."

But I see the way she looks back at me as she drags him over to introduce him to her sister, can feel the split-second of indecision as she leaves me sitting there. He doesn't know the first thing about Hadley, and she's going to let him get away with it. And I do not like that at all.

21

Hadley

I'm finishing setting the table when the doorbell rings. *Right on time.* One point for Ryan. I have no idea why I'm tallying points so early in the evening, but I try to push that thought away. One day that'll be a funny little bit about this evening, a way I tell our children about how nervous making dinner for their father made me. That's what I'm telling myself as I open the door, anyway, putting on a great big smile to greet my maybe soulmate.

"Look at you, babe." Ryan plants a kiss on my cheek as soon as the door opens, pulling me tight against him. "You're a regular June Cleaver. You've got an apron and everything."

"I don't want to get anything on my dress, obviously." I look down to see the frilly apron I'd intended to take off before I opened the door.

"It's cute, makes it look like you really cooked." He hands me a bottle of wine, and I let him breeze past me into the living room.

"I *did* cook. I invited you over for dinner, what did you

think I was going to do? Order pizza?" I stand in the doorway, trying to imagine a world where I would invite a man over for dinner and then not bother to cook anything.

"Oh." Ryan turns a bit, his face a little surprised. "I thought you were inviting me for 'dinner.'" His air quotes make me shudder a little.

"Like it was a trick to get you alone in my apartment?"

Ryan's eyebrow raises. "Was it?"

"If I wanted to invite you over for a booty call, I would have told you that. I made short ribs." Truthfully, in the back of my mind, I had been thinking about what might happen after dinner. I'm sure Ryan's getting bored with taking it slow. Having him live forty-five minutes out of town makes that a little less difficult to explain. He can't exactly spend the night here and then make it to work without some difficulty. But we both know that's an excuse I'm using to cut our nights short.

"If there's one thing I love about you, Hadley, it's your ability to be blunt." Ryan doesn't sound like he really means that. "Show me around your apartment." Already he's walking through the living room like he lives here.

"I can give you a quick tour. The ribs need to come out of the oven in a few minutes, and I've still got a salad to throw together."

"It smells great in here. Who knew you could cook?"

"Well, you haven't tasted it yet." I'm joking, but Ryan takes it as the truth.

"You worried we're going to need to order a pizza?" He fakes a big shrug. "I didn't ask you out because of your cooking."

I startle. I know he didn't think I was a contestant on *Master Chef*, but what the hell? "Why *did* you ask me out?" I'm playing with fire here, but maybe Ryan's answer will keep me from feeling the pit in my stomach that's threatening to overtake everything else.

"Seriously? Have you seen your legs?" He's not joking. "Those alone are worth that drive."

It isn't exactly sweet, but I try to pretend it is. "Let me show you around." I take his hand, hoping that will jump start some feelings, but all I can think about is how Cooper's hand felt in mine a few days ago. I try to put that memory in the back of my mind.

Ryan's not very interested until we get to the bedroom, then he's running his hands over everything, plopping down on the edge of the bed.

"Come sit next to me." He beckons me with one outstretched hand. I sit on the end of the bed, allowing my hip to touch his. "You're so shy, Hadley," he says as he leans in to kiss me.

Shy? WTF? No one in the history of my time on Earth has ever called me shy. Luckily the oven timer goes off just as Ryan's trying to ease me back onto the mattress.

"I need to pull those ribs out of the oven." I nearly jump up from the bed, separating from him in one fluid motion. "Don't want them to burn."

"Of course. Dinner first," he declares. "Let's see how you did."

Dinner doesn't go much better. Yes, everything I made is delicious, but Ryan barely seems to notice after the initial shock that I can cook wears off.

"Look, I'm not saying I have a problem with it, I'm saying there's a time and a place."

"For women to drive race cars?" I can't believe I'm having this conversation.

"Women aren't exactly known for their ability to drive, Hadley." Ryan puts another bite of salad in his mouth and chews contemplatively. "That stereotype doesn't come from nowhere."

"I think by definition a *stereotype* doesn't necessarily come from hard data, Ryan." I put a forkful of my baked potato into my mouth so forcefully I'm lucky I don't chip a tooth with my fork.

"Okay, but how many women do you know who could compete on the racing circuit? Be honest." He points his empty fork at me. "Zero, right?"

"That's how we're settling this? Contemplating the number of women I personally know who would be able to compete as racer drivers?" I hope the expression on my face shows the absurdity of this. "That's maybe the dumbest thing I've ever heard."

"Come on, surely that's not the *dumbest* thing you've ever heard. I mean, you hang around with that Cooper guy." Ryan swirls his fork around in the sauce on his plate. "I'm sure he says dumb stuff all the time. According to your sister he's not exactly a member of the brain trust."

"Mindy said that?" I can't believe my sister would say *anything* about Cooper to Ryan.

"Yeah, but he's a good ol' boy, right? I didn't expect him to be all that smart. I assumed it'd take both of you to get that project done." Ryan takes another bite of the Asian short ribs I've made for him. "These are good, by the way."

No shit those are good. The short ribs are my go-to first dinner date night at home recipe. I've tested them a million times. They are foolproof, and Ryan is showing himself to be a fool.

"Why would you think that about Cooper? He's not even from here." I go ahead and let Ryan dig the hole a little deeper.

"He's not? Honestly, sometimes I can't tell. He seems like all the guys from around here."

"He was raised in Nashville. Only here for the summers." I put another bite of potato in my mouth and chew it slowly.

"Well, Nashville's just as bad, right?" Ryan shrugs like we're both in on some joke. But if he thinks Nashville's hillbilly, what must he think about a girl who's never left Mint Springs?

"I thought you stayed in Tennessee because you liked it," I prompt. Hadn't he said that the first time we'd met?

"I do like Tennessee. Chattanooga's great, as far as mid-sized cities go, but I wouldn't want to stay there forever. I mean, the tax break is fabulous. No state income tax? Who thought that up? But long term I'd probably want to move some place with a little more culture, you know?" Ryan shrugs.

Oh, I know alright.

"You know, I think I'm getting a little bit of a headache." I massage my temples with my fingers.

"Can you take something? We haven't even had *dessert*." Ryan says the last word in the porniest way imaginable.

"I'm not sure that'll work. I think I need to go lie down. Alone." I try to act disappointed that the evening's getting cut short. "I need to be up early anyway. Cooper and I have that distillery tour, remember?"

"Ah, yes. Of course, you need to spend the day with Cooper. Wouldn't want to mess that up." Ryan pulls his napkin from his lap, chucking it onto the table. "I can stay over, if you want. To be sure you're okay." Maybe a few days ago, I would have taken Ryan up on the offer, let him stay the night, thinking he was doing it because he was a nice guy. Tonight I have my doubts.

"You don't need to do that. I'll be fine on my own. But you should get going before the migraine really sets in. Sometimes I throw up." I grimace to emphasize the horror of him witnessing such humanity from me. Predictably, it's enough to have Ryan heading for the door.

Once I turn the bolt I let out a giant sigh, leaning against the door and sliding down until I'm sitting on the floor of my empty apartment. Somehow the silence is so much better than hearing Ryan tell me all about his opinions. I take a few minutes to clean up the rest of the dishes and then tuck myself into bed, alone but not at all sad about it.

22

Cooper

"You don't have to drive every time, you know. I'm perfectly capable of doing it." Hadley crosses those long legs, and I have trouble focusing on the road. That flirty skirt is a little on the short side.

"I know. I like driving."

Hadley stiffens in the seat next to me. "Is that some kind of man thing? Like you think a woman couldn't possibly be capable of driving? Men are better at it or something?"

"Whoa, there, Hadley. Comin' in kind of hot for first thing in the morning." I look over at her angry face, arms crossed over her chest. "I've seen you drive. You're a fine driver. Never said otherwise."

"I can drive a tractor, just so you know. And a straight shift." She glares at me.

"Okay, I believe you." I'm not sure what's gotten into Hadley, but I'm hoping the entire drive isn't like this. We've got a few hours to go before we get to the first distillery on our itinerary.

"Well, you should."

"I do. Jesus, what's got you so riled up?"

Hadley's frown turns into more of a pout. "Something Ryan said last night."

Ah, great. Now I'm paying for something Hadley's new boyfriend said. There is no justice. "He criticized your driving?" He's lucky to be alive, if that's the case.

"Yes, and women drivers in general. He was joking, but..."

"But it still pissed you off." I chuckle a bit to myself. Picking a fight with Hadley over something like that is inadvisable at best. I should not be asking any questions about Hadley and her fight with Ryan. If anything, I should be turning up the radio and concentrating on the road. The long stretch of highway spooling out in front of us doesn't require all that much attention, though, so I go against my better judgment and step into the fray. "You set him straight?"

"I tried, but he thinks it's 'cute' when I get mad about things like that." Hadley's air quotes cut through the cab of the truck like claws.

"You *are* pretty cute when you're mad." My confession startles her enough to have her shutting her mouth for a second. When it transforms into a snarl, I know I've made a serious miscalculation. I might be paying for that all day, unfortunately.

Hadley shakes her head. "Why do y'all think it's okay to get women angry for no good goddamned reason? Pardon my French, but there is no other way to put it. Such a waste of time." She turns to look out the window, and I regret not keeping my mouth shut.

I clear my throat. "I can only speak for myself, but there's something about seeing a woman get kind of fiery. I don't want her to be mad at me, exactly, but I like the emotion. It gets kind of close to..." I stop myself from saying what I'd intended.

"It gets close to what?" Hadley turns back to look at me.

I let out a long breath. "To sex, Hadley. To that feeling before. Passion, I guess."

Hadley's mouth opens a bit like she's getting ready to argue. "You'd fight with a woman for that?"

"Not fight, exactly, but it's a good substitute sometimes." Now I *do* reach out to turn the radio up, letting George Strait fill the cab.

Hadley's hand comes out to lower the volume. "Seriously, Cooper. You'd start an argument? For that?"

"Not a serious argument, no. But a teasing one? Sure."

"That's crazy," Hadley huffs.

"Is it? It's a little like pulling your pigtails. I don't condone that, necessarily." I cut a sideways glance at her, the idea of Hadley in pigtails painting a less than wholesome picture in my head. "But if the choice is having you ignore me or showing me a little temper, I know what I'm choosing."

"You tease women to get attention?"

"Not all women, Hadley. Just one." This shuts her up. There is only one woman I do this absolutely juvenile thing with, and she's sitting next to me. Only Hadley Crawford reduces me to a kid on the playground.

"We aren't talking about me and you, Cooper." Hadley's voice is quiet.

"I know. And I can't speak for him. That's my immature way of doing things." I try not to squeeze the steering wheel too tightly. I might secretly want Ryan to be a jerk, but I don't want him to act like one to Hadley. He is supposed to be all the things I can't be, not an even *more* annoying version of me.

"He's not a jerk." Hadley doesn't say that as definitively as I'd like. "He wasn't too excited about our trip. I think that might have been part of it."

"I can see that." Having another man take my girlfriend on an overnight would have me tied up in knots too. This trip with Hadley has me tied up in knots, for other reasons.

"I explained it was the only way for us to see multiple places on a schedule and that we have separate rooms. I even explained it was for school." Hadley's face falls a bit. "He still wasn't convinced you don't have some kind of ulterior motive."

I can't say I'm sad to find out Ryan doesn't trust me. If the circumstances were different, I'd say he absolutely shouldn't. Hadley and I alone together would be trouble if I hadn't already decided long ago to keep Hadley at arm's length. This project is testing me, sure, but I'm determined not to cross the line. Almost kissing Hadley was as close as I can afford to get to a mistake. I need to keep my feelings in check no matter how hard they may be to fight. And they are getting damn near impossible to ignore with the two of us spending so much time together. The end of this project can't come soon enough.

We spend the day at one of the better-known distilleries, doing the tour and trying not to get tipsy with all the tasting. It's more of a packaged kind of experience, everything glossy and well-timed. I like it less because of this and, if Hadley's lack of enthusiasm's any indication, she feels the same. She's still charming everyone we come across—staff and fellow customers alike—giving everyone that big smile of hers and chatting her way through multiple drinks. We've got more than one stop, and once we're at our final destination, I'm sure I'm going to have to excuse myself for a cold shower before we head to dinner. There's only so much of Hadley smiling and cooing I can take. I love having Hadley all to myself, but watching how other people react to her still makes me feel prouder than it should. I see the way they look at me when they think Hadley's mine. Just being with her makes them think better of me than I deserve.

Luckily, she suggests we split up when we get to the hotel, so she can freshen up before dinner. I nearly run from the hotel check-in desk to get away from her, leaving her to wrangle her own bags, even if she calls me out on it later.

I shut my hotel room door behind me and turn the TV on, hoping to drown out the messages my head can't stop sending me. But no amount of mindless television watching is going to save me from my thoughts. If anything, my brain is determined to spend even more time obsessing about Hadley—I've got her laugh and smile on repeat. A shower doesn't make things any better, and neither does pulling on the outfit I've brought for our dinner tonight. This distillery's got a fancy tasting dinner—whiskeys paired with each course and reservations required. Hadley's been talking about it all week, her excitement bubbling over as we compile our data and work on our presentation. I've been looking forward to it, too, until I give myself a good look in the full-length mirror on the back of the bathroom door.

My shirt's crisp and clean, my face freshly shaved. I decided against wearing a tie, but that doesn't do anything to change the date night vibe my outfit's giving off. I could have gone more casual, I guess, but that would mean disappointing Hadley, who's been talking up this dinner experience for days. And it's supposed to be an experience—one I'm hoping to be able to recreate with my brothers at our restaurant, if I'm lucky. It isn't a time for me to pull on a pair of jeans and a band T-shirt. This is not the way to keep things casual with Hadley, though. All this looking like a couple is messing with my head. Still, I pull on my jacket and run my fingers through my hair one more time before slipping my hotel key card in my pocket.

I'm shutting my door behind me when the door of the room next to mine opens. Out steps Hadley, her usually curly hair straightened and her already dangerous body poured into a red dress that somehow shows off both her legs and her shoulders. I forget to breathe for a second as she turns to look at me. I know what I should say here—it's the opposite of everything I'm thinking. Or I should say nothing at all—ignore the fact that Hadley looks so beautiful I can feel my heart cracking in my chest? Good Lord, why does Hadley have to be so tantalizingly close? Why does she have to give me one of those smiles that knocks the wind right out of me, making every single one of my nerve endings fire at once?

"You clean up nice." Hadley's compliment shouldn't have me puffing up the way it does, but I can't seem to fight it anymore.

"You look gorgeous." I don't make it a joke, and I can't pretend to be oblivious.

Hadley ducks her head for a second, but I know she's not bashful. "Thank you."

We stand in the hallway like two kids on their way to senior prom until I manage to remember how to act. I offer her my arm. "Shall we?"

She slips her hand into the crook of my elbow, and I forget all the things I'm supposed to do. I ignore all the warning bells going off in my head and take Hadley Crawford out like I have the right to.

Like she's mine.

23

Hadley

"Oh, sweet Jesus, you have to taste this." I know I should probably lower my voice, but when something's this delicious, I have trouble with self-control. And while this filet might be the most delicious thing I've ever eaten, something pretty delicious is sitting across from me. When Cooper opens his mouth and lets me slide a bite of my steak in, I have trouble not leaning in to lick off the little bit of sauce that clings to his lower lip with my tongue.

I move my fork and let him finish chewing. The face he's making is nothing short of orgasmic, and I'm mesmerized by the way he squeezes his eyes shut before he lets out a groan I feel in some very inconvenient places.

"Take a sip of the whiskey now." I hand him my glass and he takes a sip, his eyes widening.

"The char..." He closes his eyes again. "That's so good."

"Right?" I cut another bite of the filet for myself. "The smokiness of the meat and the smokiness of the whiskey..." I bring my fingers to my lips in a chef's kiss. "Do you think you and your brothers could ever make something like this?

Please say yes so I can eat this every night." I put the morsel of meat in my mouth and slowly chew.

"I hope so. I'm not a restaurant expert, but Charlie knows how to run the front of the house. I think the key's going to be hiring the right people in the kitchen. And sourcing ingredients. I love that so much of this is local." He takes a look around the restaurant, with its candlelit tables and dark wood. "I love everything about this place, I think." His eyes come back to focus on me again. "I'm starting to think we can really do this, Hadley. That *I* can do this. Thanks for helping me get there. I'm having a good time doing this with you." His words are humble and sweet, and I feel another one of my walls start to crumble. "Do you want another bite of this pork belly?" He loads up his fork and holds it up for me.

I've already tasted everything on Cooper's plate, but I open my mouth again and let him feed me. We've been sharing everything this way all night and I'm not about to complain about the way it's made us slide our chairs closer, moving until we're nearly side by side at this tiny table. It's the most romantic place I think I've ever been, and Cooper's been opening doors and pulling out chairs for me since we met in the hotel hallway.

"You've got a little..." Cooper reaches out to cup my chin, his thumb running along my lower lip.

I suck in a sharp breath as his hand lingers there for a second. When he pulls his hand back, he slides his thumb in his mouth, and I nearly melt into a puddle right there. Cooper seems almost as shocked as I am, and we stare across the table at each other, both frozen.

"Cooper—"

"Whoa. That's cozier than I expected."

Cooper's chair scrapes the floor as he stands, awkwardly

moving away from me. Ryan stands in front of our table, an overnight bag in one hand and a confused look on his face.

I stand too, wobbling a bit on my heels. "Ryan? What are you doing here?" I don't sound anywhere as happy as I should be for getting a surprise visit from my sort-of boyfriend.

"I thought I'd drive up. Join you on your trip." He lifts his bag a fraction. "Make use of the hotel."

"Oh. Um, how nice." I make it sound like a parking ticket, but I finally manage to move close enough to embrace him. He turns his face so the kiss I intended for his cheek lands on his lips.

"This is a lot." Ryan gestures to my outfit. "Going all out for this, eh?"

I expect some kind of compliment, but he doesn't give me one.

Cooper's mouth pinches, but he stays standing. "Maybe we can pull up an extra chair or something." He looks around for our server, who's over in an instant and trying to accommodate our last-minute addition.

"Can I get something for you, sir?" She's efficient and chipper and completely unaware of the strain now dominating our table.

Ryan busies himself with the menu while I try to get myself in a better frame of mind. I should be happy he's here, should be thrilled with the effort he's made to surprise me. But I can't help but wonder if any of this is about me at all as he slides his chair closer and glares a bit at Cooper. And he's shown up to spend the night, something we haven't discussed and I haven't agreed to. Ryan's making some pretty big assumptions. His knee bumps mine, and I move to try to make a little more space; Ryan barely acknowledges it.

"I'll be right back." I stand and excuse myself. Cooper

stands too and seems shocked when Ryan doesn't do the same. I go through the front door and out onto the wide porch. I take a deep breath and pull out my phone. Mindy answers on the first ring.

"Is he there? Oh my God, were you so excited?" Mindy barely takes a breath. "I told him you'd love it."

"What are you talking about?"

"Ryan. Duh. He's there now, right? Saving you from Cooper and his stupid, scowling face." I can feel her huge grin through the phone.

"He's here, Mindy, but you should have warned me," I huff. "I wasn't really prepared for him to show up out of the blue."

"Well, now you don't have to waste more time with Cooper. You can spend time with the man you want to see, not the one you ended up stuck with." If Mindy were here, she'd have her hand up for a high five.

"It's not as easy as that, Mindy. I'm not sure how I feel about Ryan."

My confession falls on deaf ears. "That's only because Cooper gets you all twisted up, Hadley. I saw the way you two were looking at each other at the salon. You cannot be entertaining thoughts of him finally manning up and giving you some sort of relationship. He's not going to. Cooper Allen's always going to disappoint you. Ryan, on the other hand—he's perfect. Believe me."

"No one's perfect, Mindy, Ryan included." I sigh, looking up at the baby blue ceiling of this gorgeous porch. I make a mental note to tell Cooper about the ceiling.

Cooper. Poor Cooper. Stuck at the table with my...whatever Ryan is to me.

"But he's there now. Why are you talking to me? Shouldn't you be jumping his bones? Thanking him profusely for driving all the way out there to hang out in the boonies with you?"

"This isn't exactly the boonies, Mindy, and he and I aren't at the jumping bones stage yet. You know this." I shudder a little at the phrase "jumping bones."

"Then tonight could be the night. How fancy is this hotel?"

I think back to the clean white sheets and breezy balcony of my hotel room, the one *right next* to Cooper's. "It's just a hotel room. Nothing special." And there's no way I'm bringing Ryan back there, not for what Mindy has in mind. "I need to go, but we're going to have a talk about this when I get back home."

"Fine. That'll give you a chance to *thank* me."

"*Thank* you?" I sputter, but Mindy's already hung up. I'm not the only one who inherited the Crawford temper.

I make a quick stop in the ladies' room, where I give myself a little pep talk in the mirror while I reapply my lipstick. How could Ryan not have gushed over this outfit? I look damn good, and the stares I get from the other patrons as I walk through the restaurant only reinforce how fabulous I look in this dress. Fabulous with a capital "F."

One thing that is decidedly not fabulous is the general mood at our table. Ryan and Cooper are facing away from each other, staring angrily in opposite directions. Ryan's got a drink in front of him, but the atmosphere's anything but festive.

Cooper's face lights up when he sees me, but he's quick to school his features. He stands as I get closer. "I'm going to go on back to the hotel and let you and Ryan finish here."

"And miss dessert? No, Cooper," I protest. "The whole point of this trip is this dinner right here." Having Cooper leave me here with Ryan is meant to be gracious, but this is supposed to be research. Already I know Ryan won't be helpful with the flavors or care at all about the presentation. "You have to stay."

"No, you two enjoy it. We'll meet back up in the morning to plan the day." Cooper doesn't seem thrilled to be leaving, but Ryan perks up considerably.

"Hope you won't mind me tagging along tomorrow. I'd like to be able to spend some time with Hadley. Can't let you steal her for the whole weekend." There's not an ounce of mirth in Ryan's statement. He makes tomorrow sound about as appealing as a day-old egg sandwich.

"We're going to be working on this project, Ryan. I'm not sure it'll be all that fun for you." I'm trying to be diplomatic in front of Cooper. Ryan hasn't been invited to come with us tomorrow, and I'm determined to let him know how I really feel about it once we're alone.

"But I guess it'd be fun if it was just you and Cooper." Ryan's snide remark lands with a thud.

"I beg your pardon?" I stiffen and notice Cooper doing the same.

"I know all about how Cooper broke your heart, Hadley, and anyone can see he's back to string you along again. Unless you think he's serious this time. Maybe we should ask him? Cooper, why don't you tell us how you feel about Hadley?" It's a dare, and I don't know if I'm more terrified Cooper will take it or that he'll ignore it.

"I'm not trying to pull anything here, Ryan. Hadley and I are stuck together—this is work. She and I are friends, nothing more. I don't have feelings for Hadley." Cooper pushes in his chair. "I'll see you two in the morning." He's walking away before I can argue.

I start to go after him, but the appearance of our server with Ryan's dinner keeps me at the table. I watch Cooper push through the restaurant doors. Ryan seems more than placated by Cooper's speech, tucking into his pork chop before my butt even hits the chair. I know I should be, too. Cooper's told me everything I need to know. We're friends. He's not interested. It's all in black and white.

But I know something now that I can't ignore, something Ryan would have missed even if he had been paying attention. When Cooper was reassuring him that he feels nothing for me, his eye twitched.

24

Cooper

I try to keep my hands from balling into fists as I walk away from the table. As much as I want to turn back around, I keep moving forward until I'm out in the parking lot. Once I'm safely in the truck I give the steering wheel a good pounding, banging my fists, like that's going to solve anything. The truck's done nothing wrong, but since I can't exactly pummel Ryan, this is my only option. That son of a bitch deserves what the truck's getting and so much more.

What can Hadley possibly see in that guy? It's a familiar feeling I've got settling in my chest. It happens every time I run across Hadley with another man, especially one who's nowhere near deserving of her. I know I can't have her, and it's selfish to have even been thinking about it, but her ending up with a man who can't be bothered to stand when she walks in the room? One who thinks her plugging away to get her education is *cute*? Hell no.

That's what he'd told me when I tried to make conversation while Hadley was gone. After a minute of silence so thick you could have cut it with my steak knife, I'd tried to be friendly. Hadley likes him, and he seems determined to stick around—hell, he showed up unannounced and uninvited all the way out here just to see her—so I made an effort. Small talk's never been my strong suit, but I tried. Lord knows I'm regretting it now.

"You and Hadley getting serious?" It was none of my business but I asked it anyway, almost hoping he'd say no.

"Nah, she's good fun, though. You should know that."

I'd stiffened at what seemed like a dig. Maybe it was meant for me, but it sure felt like he was aiming that arrow at Hadley.

"She's a good girl." I sipped on my whiskey, trying to act like it was the most reasonable thing in the world for Hadley's boyfriend to insinuate something like that right in front of me.

"Well, she's a looker, that's for sure."

"But there's more to Hadley than that," I'd argued. "Sure, she's pretty, but she's smart too. She got into Harvard. And you have to be proud of how she's managed to finish her degree while working a full-time job."

"If you can call what she does a job, I guess. And, yeah, it's great she's taking classes. It's cute how she's so into it. But she hasn't finished yet, so let's hold off on the celebration, you know?" Ryan had raised a knowing eyebrow at me, and I'd wanted to knock that smug look right off his face.

Cute? I'd seen red. I'm so damn proud of Hadley for not giving up on college. If she were anything close to mine, you can bet I'd be shouting that from every rooftop in Mint Springs. Her work not being a *job*? What the hell did that mean? And then Hadley walked back in and I'd had to play nice. Had to leave her there with him when everything in me wanted to shepherd her out of there with me.

Where she belongs.

But she doesn't. I've made sure of that, treating her in ways that rival Ryan. Guilt courses through me. Hadley doesn't deserve any of this. I've gone about it all wrong. My heart lurches in my chest. By pushing Hadley away, I've pushed her into the arms of a complete asshole.

The drive to the hotel is short—too short to get rid of any of the bad feelings that are now smothering me. They cover up all the good I'd had before, when Hadley and I'd been together. I curse myself as I put the truck in park and stomp into the hotel lobby. There's a little store there and I go in, determined to find the strongest whiskey I can find. There's nothing as nice as the liquor we tasted today, and I regret not snagging a bottle on my way out of the last distillery. That'd be better to drown my sorrows with than this budget stuff, but maybe the burn'll remind me of how I got here in the first place. I don't deserve anything smooth right now.

I kick open the door to my hotel room and realize that in a few minutes I'm going to be treated to the sounds of Hadley and Ryan on the other side of our shared wall. There's no way this hotel's walls are anything less than paper-thin, if today's luck is any indication. I'll be able to hear every moan and sigh once they get back from the dinner I made sure I paid for before I left the restaurant. But I guess that's the kind of penance a man like me deserves— hearing the woman I've always pined for with another man might be what I need to realize how badly I've fumbled things with Hadley.

I pull the plastic from the bottle and grab one of the glasses from next to the TV. I don't bother with ice—that would mean leaving my room and potentially running into Hadley and Ryan in the hallway. My imagination's already provided me with a very vivid idea of what they might be doing in the elevator on the way up here. I don't need to confirm it.

I pour myself more whiskey than I need and turn on the television. I push the buttons on the remote with deadly force, but still manage to get to the sports channel. I don't care who's playing—hell, I don't even care what sport's on. I need some background noise to drown out anything that might be happening in the hall or the room next to mine. And to silence the voice in my head that keeps telling me to go back to the restaurant, throw Hadley over my shoulder, and get her as far away from that idiot as I can.

I toss back the amber liquid in my glass. The whiskey does burn, but that's no surprise. What does surprise me is the sound of a knock on the door. I get up off the couch, ready to apologize for the noise I must be making with the TV, and open the door. But it's not hotel management standing there on the other side.

It's Hadley.

25

Hadley

It isn't every day you're confronted with the undeniable truth about something. Most days, I barely get a blip of excitement, much less the kind of information that rocks you to the core. But tonight, watching Cooper walk away, I can't pretend I didn't notice it.

His eye twitched.

Cooper said he didn't have feelings for me, and then he did the one thing he always does when he's not telling the truth. Maybe no one else would have noticed, but I saw it clear as day and that one little muscle spasm has changed everything. Ryan's cutting into his pork chop, unaware that I'm now weighing what to do next, unaware of what he's accidentally forced Cooper to tell me.

"Why did you drive all the way out here?" My question has Ryan looking up from his plate, his eyes meeting mine.

"To see you, obviously." He puts a bite of mashed potatoes in his mouth and shrugs.

"It had nothing to do with Cooper?" I already know the answer to this. He'd basically challenged Cooper to confirm there was something more than research going on tonight.

"Your sister did fill me in on a few things—things I would have thought you'd have told me yourself. At least Mindy thinks I deserve to know you and Cooper slept together."

I am going to strangle my sister. "Why would I have told you anything about that?"

"Oh, I don't know, Hadley, maybe because a man doesn't like for his girlfriend to go on trips with an ex-lover, especially one she carried a torch for for years. It was years, right?" The angry way Ryan asks has me sitting up straight.

"I don't see what that has to do with now."

"Look, you live in a small town. I get it. You've probably slept with half the guys in Mint Springs. I'd merely like a heads-up when you're going to be spending time with one of the more significant ones. Even if it turns out he's a loser. That only seems fair." He takes another bite of pork chop. "Especially once you start sleeping with me."

I take a long look at him—the sandy blond hair, the eyes I'd initially thought were so kind. I have misjudged Ryan. Really, really misjudged him. And he's here thinking he's going to be spending the night with me.

Nope.

I might have been hoping Ryan was something else—someone else—but he's showing me who he really is.

I move my napkin off my lap and place it on the table, scoot my chair back, and try to stand up with as much dignity as I can muster.

"Goodbye, Ryan."

"Where are you going? Bathroom again?" He looks amused.

"I'm leaving." I don't bother with more of an explanation, just turn away and walk out of the restaurant. The fact that he doesn't follow me tells me plenty. Cooper would never have let me walk away like that.

Cooper.

When the door swings open, I can tell I'm not who he was expecting to see. He's still in his dress shirt, but he's lost the jacket. His shirttails are out, and he's undone a few extra buttons so I've got a clear view of his neck and the top of his chest as he leans out, looking down the hallway toward the elevator.

"What are you doing here?" Cooper scans the hall. "Where's Ryan?" His hair is standing up all over the place, like he's been running his hands through it.

"He's gone, I think." I run my hands nervously over the tiny clutch I shoved my lipstick and hotel key card into earlier in the night.

"Gone? Gone where?" Cooper's eyes search my face. "I don't understand."

"I left him at the distillery. Can I come in?" I'm starting to feel too exposed standing out here in the hall. I doubt Ryan's going to come looking for me, but if he does, in front of Cooper's room isn't necessarily the place I want him to find me.

Cooper moves away from the door, gesturing with an arm for me to come in. The television is louder than I'd like for this conversation, but Cooper turns the volume down as he moves into the center of the room. Behind him basketball goes on as usual, despite the pounding of my heart in my chest.

"I'm sorry about tonight...about Ryan showing up like that."

"You don't need to apologize, Hadley, you didn't do anything wrong." Cooper's mouth twists into a grimace. "But I gotta be honest, I don't know what you see in him. Maybe I don't know all the facts and maybe he's got some charm I can't understand, but Hadley, he's not good enough for you. I know it isn't my place and it's none of my business, but I've been sitting here drinking, trying to work out in my head how you can possibly be with him. He's not enough for you, and he doesn't even know how not enough he is."

I stare open-mouthed at Cooper.

"See? I should have kept my mouth shut. I'm sorry." He runs his hands through his hair, leaving his hands behind his head as he paces in front of me. "Never could leave well enough alone when it comes to you."

"You lied tonight."

"What?" Cooper stops walking. "When did I lie?"

"When Ryan asked you about how you felt about me. You lied." I try to keep calm, to keep my breathing steady. Cooper could deny everything, but I know what I saw.

"This isn't going to help anything, Hadley." He shakes his head. "We can't go muddying things up right now."

"So, I was right?" I can scarcely believe what I'm hearing.

"It doesn't matter how I feel about you. This,"—Cooper gestures between us—"isn't good for you either."

"How about you let me be the judge of that?" I take two steps forward and close the distance between us, reach for the edges of Cooper's open shirt, and pull him toward me.

Then I go ahead and kiss the living daylights out of him.

Cooper

Hadley Crawford is kissing me.

Hadley Crawford is kissing *me*.

She's *kissing* me? No, no, no. I already know this isn't something I can let go on for long, but I can't bring myself to pull away from her. Hadley's like every perfect summer memory—easily ruined by the present. And I'm sure to ruin this, even if this feels so right right now. She groans a little and opens her mouth, melts against me a little more. Good Lord, I'd almost forgotten how perfectly we fit together. Hadley presses against me, and I can't get enough.

I can't have that though, so I work to extract myself from her roaming hands and soft, warm mouth.

"Hadley, we can't."

She blinks up at me. "Why not?"

"Because nothing's changed. I know I just tried to make the case that Ryan's not good enough for you, but that doesn't mean I'm any better." I'm cupping her cheeks when I should be moving to the other side of the room, when I should be escorting her out into the hall and depositing her in her own room next door.

"Cooper." Hadley's tone is no nonsense. "We aren't going to the courthouse to make things official. We're just kissing."

"Right *now* we're just kissing, but you know we could never stick to just kissing." I don't mean for the memory to make her smile or for it to settle in my chest the way it does. Hadley Crawford, warm and willing in my arms, was always like coming home. Thinking about it now, I know we were too young to feel the things I thought I was feeling. Hadley was barely out of high school, and I had a few years of college under my belt but not much to show for it. We were babies.

Still.

The memory of those nights with Hadley, sneaking away from my brothers and the rest of our friends assembled down by the river, made it even sweeter. Hadley was all mine, even if it did mean having to use the hayloft. I run my thumbs over Hadley's cheeks and look deep into her corn-flower eyes. That warmth is still there, even after everything I've done to try to cool things down.

When I press my lips to hers, I try to be reverent. Chaste. I'm kissing her for the last time, getting ready to restate my case for the two of us to go our separate ways. I might be thinking about her on the other side of the wall for the rest of the night, but I won't have crossed a line. Everything so far can be taken back. Hadley and I haven't done anything yet we can't come back from.

But Hadley didn't get the memo, and as soon as she opens her mouth and slides her tongue against mine, I forget the original plan. She's the most delicious thing I've ever tasted—spicy and sweet like the whiskey we've been drinking all day. I deepen the kiss, and Hadley presses back up against me, eagerly wrapping her arms around my neck. I slide a hand around to the back of her head and thread my fingers through her hair. The strands are silky, straight where they're usually curly. I don't mind her hair this way, but I'm wishing for the wavy curls I used to run my fingers through.

"Did I tell you you look beautiful tonight?" I ask it against the skin of her neck, my tongue tasting its way toward her collarbone.

"Not in so many words," Hadley murmurs.

"Well, you do, but then you always look beautiful." I take the chance to tell her while I've got it.

Hadley scoffs, pulling back to look me in the eye. "You don't need to flatter your way into anything, Cooper. I'm already here." Her hands travel lower down my back. "Less talking."

I get a lungful of her perfume as I lean in closer. "But don't you think we should maybe talk about—"

Hadley shuts me up with a blistering kiss. This has always been a reliable way to keep me quiet, and I'm guessing she remembers. Her mouth against mine has me forgetting all the reasons I'd told myself this wouldn't work. *What was I worried about? Whoosh, there goes all of that.*

I run my hands over Hadley's body, letting them come to rest on her ass. I pull her tight against me and she sighs, grinding a little against me. I've been fighting my body's reaction to her forever now, and it feels like absolute freedom to let all that go. It's been years since I've been able to let myself think of Hadley like this, much less follow through with anything.

Hadley slides her hands to my chest and gets to work on

the buttons of my shirt, sliding the whole thing off my shoulders as soon as the last one's undone.

"Oh, hello to *this*." Hadley pulls away from me and lets her eyes rake over my naked chest. Months and months of farm work have me fitter than I've ever been. She runs her fingers along the ridges of my abdomen, and goosebumps rise on my entire body. I close my eyes and lean into the feeling of having Hadley's hands on me again. Her touch is light—teasing—and it's like a balm after imagining her with someone else.

Her lips come down softly on my shoulder as she eases the shirt off my arms and drops it on the floor. I turn my head toward her, nuzzling against her. She's reaching for my belt buckle but I cover her hand with mine.

"Am I the only one getting naked here?"

"Who said we were getting naked?" Hadley turns her mouth toward mine and I swallow whatever words she's getting ready to say.

When we pull apart again, I'm hard as a fencepost and well aware Hadley can feel every inch. Her palm glides over the front of my pants, and I groan a little. Hadley was always a master at making me work for it, and I don't think things have changed much, if her moves tonight are any indication. She takes two steps back, keeping her eyes locked with mine. She reaches back and her zipper hisses. She slides one strap and then the other down over her shoulders, letting the front of her dress slowly slip lower. Hadley lets it fall and it puddles at her feet. When she steps out of it, impossibly high heels still on her feet and a scrap of material too tiny to be called panties on her lower half, I let out a low whistle.

"Better?" Her breasts rise and fall as she speaks.

"No bra?" I'm not complaining, although it is a testament to my own willpower that I hadn't noticed it sooner.

Hadley doesn't answer; instead she moves forward and wraps her arms back around me. I let my thumbs skim along her back, hungry to touch all of her. There was a time when I knew Hadley's body well, didn't have to guess about a thing when it came to pleasing her. But that was years ago, and I'm looking forward to finding out what she loves now. I slide my hands around and cup her breasts, pinching the nipples a bit. Hadley tilts her head back and sucks in a sharp breath between her teeth. That's apparently one thing that still works.

Hadley's hand snakes down the front of my pants, and it's my turn to gasp. She's never been shy, and her grip on me is firm. She pumps me a few times, and I'm desperate to get out of these pants. I fumble around trying to toe off my shoes and socks without breaking contact with all the parts of Hadley I'm so thoroughly enjoying.

Hadley laughs but takes pity on me, using her free hand to make short work of my belt and then the button of my dress pants. She keeps her other hand where it was, continuing to torture me with the slow up and down of her fingers wrapped tight around my cock.

I all but dance right out of my pants and have to remind myself to slow down. This isn't a race, and I can't afford to rush through what might be my only chance to be with Hadley. Who knows what will happen once we're outside this hotel room and back in the real world? I push those thoughts away and focus on the way Hadley's skin feels against mine and the noises she's making as I walk her back to the bed. Once her knees hit the edge, I lower her down. Hadley's face is even with my erection, and she leans forward, determined to put her mouth on me. I imagine those lips wrapped around my shaft and know I won't last two seconds if I let her take the lead.

"No, no," I chastise, pulling back a bit. "Ladies first." My hands glide along her ribs down to the thin straps around her hips. I tuck my thumbs there and pull, baring her to me as I lower myself to my knees.

27

Hadley

Cooper's face between my legs is as surprising to me as it would be to anyone. I had thought confronting him would end up in an uncomfortable conversation. Right now, though, I'm *extremely* comfortable stretched out on his bed. I thread my fingers through his hair and grind against his mouth. I always marveled at the way he could work my body. I had thought that was the way it would be forever. Unfortunately, not every man is Cooper Allen in the bedroom. Lucky for me, I've ended up getting another opportunity to see if he's everything I remember.

So far, so good.

I'm panting as Cooper groans like he's eating the most delicious thing ever, bringing me so close to exploding I'm clutching the comforter in a death grip.

I guess we didn't skip dessert after all.

I have never been a quiet girl and coming is no exception to that rule. The evidence of my orgasm bounces off the walls of the hotel room. You can probably hear me two floors down, I'm moaning so loud. Cooper doesn't stop until

I'm nothing but jelly, babbling his name as he kisses his way back up my body to claim my mouth again.

"That was two old moves and one new one." Cooper winks at me. "From what I can tell you liked all three."

"I thought you barely remembered me." I raise an eyebrow. "How would you know which moves I used to like?" I should probably rake Cooper over the coals a bit for that admission, but I'm already letting my fingers walk all over his abs.

Cooper looks at the ceiling and lets out a tortured breath. "I never forgot you, Hadley."

I pump a fist in the air. "I knew it! Several people are going to owe me big apologies."

"Well, don't go telling that all over town. It makes me look like an ass."

I give him a look.

"Okay, *more* of an ass. I'm sorry." Cooper runs a hand through his hair. "How could I forget you?" His eyes soften, and I forget all the times he's made me furious, all the times he's been—his words, not mine—an ass.

"I was pretty sure you couldn't." I smooth the errant bits of hair back down, using that as an excuse to keep touching him. "But we can talk about that later." I raise up on my elbows and press my lips to his. I should force an apology out of him right now, should demand he explain everything, but I'm distracted by Cooper's dick still poking me in the side. If I wanted to get even, I could start by ignoring that obviously very pressing need. I could get up, pull my dress back on, and walk out the door. That would teach Cooper a lesson.

But my need for revenge is trumped by my need for another orgasm. I roll on top of him, still kissing him like a fool. Cooper kisses me back, and before I know it, we're all hands and mouths and groans again—until I notice one tiny detail.

I'm still wearing my shoes.

I tilt my head back and laugh.

"Not sure if I should be offended," Cooper says as he moves his mouth over my left nipple. "Been a while since I've had a woman laugh right in the middle like that." He manages to look up at me without losing his hold on my breast.

I gesture toward my feet, a giant smile plastered on my face.

Cooper leans back but immediately returns to tracing all over my chest with his tongue. "I was hoping you could leave those on."

When I wake up in the morning, my face still pressed to Cooper's chest, I get ready for the inevitable backtracking. Cooper's made it clear for the past few months that there isn't anything between us. Eye twitching aside, there must be something that made him make that decision in the first place, and I doubt one night of extremely aerobic sex is going to wipe that slate clean.

I try to slide away from Cooper slowly, hoping to escape to my own room before he wakes up. At least when I have to face him in an hour or so, I'll be wearing clean underwear. I'm almost positive Dolly never said anything profound about clean panties, but I'm pretty sure she'd see the wisdom in them. Especially in a situation like this.

I'm easing myself off the mattress when Cooper's arm shoots out to grab me, pulling me back down in an uncoordinated heap on top of him. He wraps his arms around me and holds me close

"You weren't running out on me, were you?" Cooper's lips tickle the shell of my ear.

"Not running, exactly. Trying to give you a little space, that's all."

Cooper releases me. "You want space?" His brow furrows.

"I thought you'd want some, maybe." I prop up on an elbow. "I know this was a one-time thing. There's no need to make it awkward."

Cooper's hand reaches out and lands on my bare hip, this thumb stroking the skin there. "You want this to be a one-time thing?"

"I don't know what I want, Cooper, and I don't think you do either." That's a lie, but I don't have a tell like Cooper does. I know I want more time with Cooper, and not only because he's refreshed my memory about his bedroom skills. Now that he's acting more like the boy I remembered, he's a man I'd like to get to know better.

"I know I don't want to leave this bed quite yet." That hand dips a little lower. "And that I'd like to take you out for breakfast, possibly lunch, if we ever make it to the next distillery today. I'd also like to keep doing all those things once we're home."

I consider this. Cooper Allen and I would be...dating? I furrow my brow and search his face for a sign that he's only kidding. When he doesn't even crack a smile, I feel all those old hopes and dreams start to resurface again—the ones that used to involve Cooper as my white knight. *Not so fast, Hadley.* This time we're taking it slow. Making sure before we give our heart away.

"Hmmm. I'll let you take me to breakfast but I'm paying

for lunch, and we'll see about how we feel once we're back in Mint Springs." I try to sound confident, like a woman who isn't actually holding her heart in her hand.

"That's a start," Cooper says, rubbing a hand over the stubble on his face. "But you forgot about the first thing I mentioned." He trails the fingers of his other hand down between my legs. "What do you say to staying a little longer in this bed?"

"You think you can make that worth my while?" I'm as saucy as I can be with Cooper's fingers already sliding through my obvious agreement.

"I'll do my best."

28

Cooper

I ride high on that wave of optimism for the next week, trying my best to keep the voices in my head at bay. There are plenty of chances for them to remind me how easily things can fall apart with Hadley. Working on this project gives her plenty of opportunities to see my stupid. It's on display constantly as we read articles and start to write the parts of our business plan. The only thing saving me is how easily distracted Hadley is when we're together. She's told me she doesn't have any expectations, but I watch for signs anyway. I'm attached to Hadley in a way I never should have allowed myself to be. I'm not trying to hurt her again.

"I think a regular presentation's going to be too boring, don't you think?" Hadley chews on the end of her pencil. Her hair's a mess, and she's still technically in her pajamas. Although she'd have to admit she didn't wear them for long last night, and she's only recently slipped them back on to have a cup of coffee with me at her kitchen table. I lobbied for naked breakfast but Hadley's got her standards.

"We're limited, though, with what we can do if it's all

online." I do not want to ruin my morning thinking about how much we have left to do before the due date. The work is piling up and only Hadley's helpful brain is currently saving me. Our discussions about the class readings and lectures are all that's keeping me afloat.

"But we could come up with something really great. We're creative." Hadley takes a sip of her coffee, and I try not to grin at the way she's already getting excited.

"I don't think we should make it too complicated, Hadley. We've already got plenty to do without adding fireworks."

Hadley gives me a shove with her shoulder. "I'm not talking about fireworks. I'm talking about trying to make it the kind of presentation your brothers will listen to—maybe even be so blown away they agree to start our distillery right then."

"*Our* distillery?" There she goes again. I try not to sweat. Hadley's just being cute, not planning our wedding.

"We've been over this. I'm not going to let you get all the glory." She winks. "Think about the presentation, though. It's all over video chat, so we couldn't have anything too fancy. But maybe we could prerecord some parts to play as we explain things. We could do it at Eddie's—that'd be interesting."

"I don't think broadcasting from Eddie Mack's is going to get us an A." I finish my coffee and reach over to pull Hadley into my lap. I'm hoping I can distract her with a few well-placed kisses. I didn't test the stability of this table, but I'm pretty sure I can make it work in a pinch.

Hadley turns around and ends up straddling me, her hands in my hair and her mouth on mine. I know she can feel my erection through the cotton of my boxer briefs— neither one of us is wearing enough to hide the fact that I'm more interested in spreading Hadley out in between our coffee cups than talking about our presentation. I palm her right breast and then her left, feeling her nipples pebble underneath the thin cotton fabric of her tank top. She leans in and I start my way down her neck, dragging my lips along her skin.

A knock at the door has us both jumping.

"You expecting anyone?" It is almost ten in the morning, but it's Sunday, so that still feels too early for a surprise visit from someone.

"No." Hadley climbs off me, and I miss the warmth of her body immediately.

"You can't answer the door like that," I protest as she moves through the living room. "At least put on some pants."

"You put on some pants," Hadley tosses over her shoulder at me. "Actually, don't you dare do that. I'll be back in two seconds."

I help myself to another cup of coffee. I pour the liquid into my mug and am about to stir in some sugar when I hear a voice I do not want to face in my underwear.

Mindy Crawford.

I freeze as Hadley's big sister charges into the room, already yelling something at me I can barely understand.

"Mindy, you cannot bust in here and start yelling at Cooper." Hadley tries to defend me, but it's no use. Mindy hates me for the way I've treated Hadley, and she'd be right to feel that way. I recognize I probably deserve every last insult she's about to hurl at me. I just wish I was a little more covered up for this confrontation.

"Oh, I can do whatever I want when it comes to him," Mindy yells. "Is this why you stopped seeing Ryan? Because you started up something stupid with Cooper? Hadley, for the love of all things holy, what are you thinking? Does Mama know?" Mindy shakes her head.

"Why don't I leave you two alone while I—"

Mindy points a finger at me. "Don't you move, Cooper Allen. I'm nowhere near done talking to you."

"And you." She turns toward Hadley. "You promised you'd babysit. I'm guessing you've forgotten." Mindy gives Hadley's tank top and tiny cotton shorts a glare. "Am I supposed to leave Caleb here in this whorehouse?"

"Whoa, hold on there." I can't let Mindy get away with calling Hadley names, even if they are sisters.

Hadley silences me with a raised hand. "Mindy, you cannot come in here and say things like that. I'm a grown woman, and I can make decisions for myself. Cooper is here, and he is my guest and you'll treat him that way. I did forget about promising to watch Caleb for you, but I'm not about to keep him if you're going to talk to me like that."

Mindy sputters. She's used to having people back down, but I can imagine that doesn't happen much with Hadley. She glares at me again. "The only reason I'm going to leave him with you is that I'm stuck. Mama can't watch him and neither can Mimi, and I've got to go to this church thing with Devin. It's no kids allowed." I swear Mindy looks like she might cry.

"Come on, Mindy. It'll be fine. Where *is* Caleb?" Hadley looks past her sister into the living room.

"Oh! I left him in the car," Mindy rushes out to grab her child, and I let my mouth hang open.

"Mother of the year right there, folks." I shake my head.

"Be nice," Hadley pleads. "She's going through a rough time."

I mimic zipping my lip, although I doubt I'll be able to

stay that way for long. I can quickly see my morning plans for Hadley and this kitchen table evaporating.

The harder, meaner version of Hadley comes back into the house, slamming the front door behind her. Hadley gives me a warning look and I try to act innocent, which is surprisingly difficult in only boxers.

"There he is!" Hadley exclaims once her nephew's in the room with us. She reaches out her arms and Caleb climbs into them, snuggling up against her.

Mindy comes over to the table and deposits a giant canvas bag in front of me. "Couldn't even have bothered to grab some clothes while I was gone?" She looks mad enough to spit.

"Didn't want you to miss another chance to get a good look," I drawl with a wink, and Mindy fumes.

"He'll get dressed in a minute so we can all play, right Cooper?" Hadley doesn't look at me, keeps her eyes and her big smile focused on Caleb.

"I don't think I have time to play today, Hadley. Might need to leave you and Caleb to have all that fun without me." Me, babysitting? That's a nope.

"That's not what you told me earlier." Hadley feigns innocence. "You seemed like you had all day to play."

"I'm going to leave before I puke," Mindy interjects. "I'll be back around two. Everything you need is in the bag." She kisses Caleb on the head. "Be good for Aunt Hadley," she whispers into his hair. Behind his back, she gives me the finger.

"Don't you worry," Hadley says, more to Caleb than to Mindy. "We are going to have so much fun today."

29

Hadley

"Not too high!" I admonish.

"Caleb and I are going to have to disagree with you on that, Hadley." Cooper gives my nephew another push, and Caleb squeals with delight.

"He's breakable, Cooper, and if you break him, we're going to have to deal with Mindy." I try to look as stern as I can, hands on hips, mouth in a firm, almost angry line, but it's hard to keep from smiling when there's a scene like that in front of you.

"This tough guy?" Cooper asks, and Caleb grins from ear to ear. "This guy can go high on the swings." He pushes again, and Caleb gives another gleeful shout.

"For two more minutes he can, then we need to get in the car to meet my sister." It's almost one, and Caleb could probably use a cat nap after all the excitement we've had today.

The park was a great choice after I convinced Cooper to put on some pants and spend the day with me and Caleb. Luckily, my nephew's pretty easygoing as far as toddlers go, so he's spent most of the morning smiling and telling Cooper all about his dinosaurs in that rambling way of his. He's very into dinosaurs, and even though he's only three, Caleb has plenty to say about them. Cooper's been more patient than I would have thought possible, participating in what feels like a million battles of the green dino versus the blue dino since Mindy left us in charge.

Cooper's a natural with Caleb, lifting him gently out of the bucket swing once he slows it down. Those tiny arms raise up, and I can feel my heart melting. Cooper sets him on the ground, and Caleb's chubby little hand reaches for one of Cooper's. They walk back to where I'm waiting at one of the picnic tables, Caleb talking nonstop. Cooper leans down, nodding his head like he can understand everything my nephew's saying and he's in total agreement.

"Caleb and I were talking on our way over," Cooper says as he helps Caleb climb up onto one of the benches, "and we haven't had any ice cream at all today. Not any."

"I see. And this is a problem because...?" I look between their two faces—Caleb's hopeful one and Cooper's slightly amused one—waiting for an answer.

"We think every day should have ice cream, and so far, this one doesn't." Cooper leans back a bit like he's argued a rock-solid case.

"Interesting. What do you suggest we do about that then?"

Cooper opens his mouth, but Caleb answers me instead, "Get ice cream."

"We don't have a lot of time before we're supposed to meet your mama, Caleb." I'm pretty sure I should be encouraging Caleb to fall asleep on the drive home, not filling him with sugar.

"We can swing by the Dairy Whip. Go through the drive-thru." Cooper's as invested as Caleb.

I pretend to mull it over, but I know I'm no match for *both* those pleading faces. Cooper and Caleb high-five when I nod yes and then we're chasing my nephew all the way back to the car. Cooper buys him the biggest cone available and then takes it from him once Caleb nods off in the car.

"Now you're going to have to eat that," I laugh as ice cream drips down Cooper's forearm.

"You can help me," he suggests, pointing the cone toward me.

"I'm trying to drive," I protest, working to keep my eyes on the road.

"I can feed it to you." Cooper's eyes are full of mischief. When he moves the ice cream cone toward me again he lets some of the cold confectionery drip onto my cheek.

"Cooper!"

At the next stoplight he kisses it off me.

"You want to explain exactly what you're doing?" Mindy's parked at my kitchen table, sipping on a cup of coffee.

"What do you mean?" I grab a glass from the cupboard in front of me and turn on the tap. I take my time filling my glass with water, so I don't have to face Mindy's judgmental stare.

"You know what I mean. You had a great guy on the hook, Hadley, and now you're sleeping with Cooper Allen? After everything he's done?"

"You make it sound like he's a murderer." I take a gulp of my water.

"Maybe he didn't kill anyone, but he broke your heart.

Did he ever give you an explanation for that? For why he acted like he didn't remember anything when he walked back into town?" Mindy regards me over the rim of her coffee cup.

"He apologized for that." He did. Yes, we were naked and, yes, it wasn't particularly enlightening, but it was an apology all the same. I don't need to tell Mindy the specifics.

"And you accepted." Mindy seems to consider this. "Of course you did."

I don't like Mindy's tone, but I'm not about to ask her to explain that crack to me. "I did. How long of a nap does Caleb usually take?"

"Probably depends on how hard he played. Normally it's maybe an hour, but it could be longer since you took him to the park." Mindy settles herself into her chair, apparently planning on staying a while. "And he'll be wide awake at bedtime."

No good deed goes unpunished around here, that's for sure.

"Cooper and I thought it'd be better than watching TV." I shouldn't feel the need to defend myself here. I was doing Mindy a favor, after all. Watching Caleb isn't really a chore, but she's still lucky I agree to do it.

"Oh, you and Cooper? Glad to know he was so helpful." Sarcasm drips from Mindy's lips.

"He was very helpful. We had a great time." I smile at the memory of Cooper and Caleb going down the slide together.

Mindy rolls her eyes. "I hope you weren't too handsy in front of Caleb. I don't want to have to explain that."

"What are you talking about? Of course we kept our hands to ourselves. You think we'd mess around in front of a toddler?" I consider getting in a jab about how it would be nice for Caleb to have seen some affection, but I know that's going too far. Whatever's gotten into Mindy isn't completely about Cooper. "How was your thing with Devin?"

Mindy's eyes get a little misty. "It was fine." She swirls the coffee in her cup. "He's distracted by work is all."

"Did today make any of that better?" I know there's much more to *any of that* than Devin's work schedule, but I try not to pry.

"It didn't, I don't think." Mindy's quiet. "But we aren't talking about me. What happened with Ryan? He seemed to tick all the boxes."

"I think he was good on paper, but maybe not really a great choice for me. You know how sometimes things look great on the surface, but then they're not so perfect underneath?"

Mindy gives me a sad smile. "I do."

"Ryan's like that. For another woman he might be perfect but...he didn't even compliment my outfit the other night when he showed up and, let me tell you, I looked incredible."

That gets a genuine smile out of Mindy. "I'm sure you 'bout burned the place down."

"A five-alarm fire for sure." I laugh, thinking about how hot it got later once I had the dress off. I keep all of that to myself.

"I'm only trying to look out for you, Hadley. You've always got such big plans, and I don't want you to get swept up in this Cooper thing and forget those. I know how long it took you to get over him the first time. I'm only hoping to keep you from heartache. When it comes to him you accept whatever he'll give instead of everything you're worth."

"I'm fine, Mindy. Really. I'm going into it with my eyes

wide open this time. Cooper and I are having a good time, and I'm not expecting anything more than that."

Mindy's expression says she doubts this, but I'm rescued by the sound of Caleb waking up in my bedroom. There's no more talk of Cooper once he's up and running around again. But what else is there to say, really? I've got my feelings for Cooper under control.

For now.

30

Hadley

When I come in to work on Monday morning, I expect the third degree. There's no way Mindy kept what she saw to herself, and even if she's only working a few shifts a week now, I'm sure she's told all the stylists I've thrown Ryan over for Cooper. This would be bad enough if the other women were able to keep things to themselves, but unless you're a client, the ladies of Hot House Flowers cannot keep a secret. The worst offenders? My mama and Mimi.

So I'm not all that surprised when I go to open the salon and find the two of them seated at the ancient kitchen table in the break room. Mimi's in a sparkly vest that would look fine on the Grand Ole Opry stage and Mama's still in her bathrobe and kitten-heeled slippers.

"Did you drive over here like that?" I gasp. "Mama, you are nearly naked."

"I spent the night at Mimi's. I was getting ready to put my face on when I heard the most interesting story." My mother gives me one of her surprised faces, and I know I'm in for a long morning. "Your sister called early, but you know she's up early with that baby and all. Woke me up and then started telling me something about you and Cooper Allen, of all people. I told your grandmother and we both hightailed it right over."

My grandma nods, the fringe on her vest swaying with the movement. "I thought maybe Mindy'd been drinking, but it seems she's sober as a judge this morning, which is good, because drunk before eight in the morning is never a good thing."

"No, ma'am," I agree. "But I don't really have time to talk. I need to get set up to open. And, Mama, you don't want people to start trickling in while you're still dressed like that." Crawford women might not always be ladies, but we try to at least look presentable. My mother is never without lipstick, so you know bare-faced is not the way she likes to greet anyone.

"That can wait, Hadley. Tell us what we want to know." Mimi can be extremely frightening when she wants to be— it's how she kept my mama in line growing up. She passed that skill down to my mother, so now I'm faced with two threatening faces and nowhere to run.

"There's nothing to tell, really." I start to pull out the things we'll need for the day and set up the shampooing station.

"Mindy didn't make it sound like nothing." Mama shakes one slippered foot, the pink feathers bouncing. She folds her hands on the table and waits. Mimi does the same.

"What did Mindy tell you, exactly?" Maybe she hasn't told them enough to keep me from bending the truth a little. This whatever it is with Cooper's too new to have my mother and Mimi in it just yet.

"That she came over to drop off Caleb and found you

and Cooper in your underwear." My mother clutches the neck of her robe like some scandalized Victorian lady.

"I had forgotten I'd volunteered to watch Caleb for her," I confess.

"I can understand why," Mimi says, and I catch her giving me a subtle wink. "He probably screwed that all right out of you. Did you even know what day it was?"

"Mimi! You cannot say things like that, especially if Cooper's around." I'm prepared to beg to keep my grandmother from opening her mouth and letting that particular sentiment come falling out again.

"Well, some things make a little more sense now." Mama looks like she's doing addition in her head, and I don't like that one bit. "He has been hanging around more, and you two have been doing things together without those brothers of his or Lily. That can only mean one thing."

"Screwing," Mimi announces.

"I beg your pardon." We're going to have to wash Mimi's mouth out with soap. "We have not been screwing."

My mother raises an eyebrow.

"Not until very recently, anyway. Not that it's any of your business."

"You expect us to believe you were spending all that time with Cooper and nothing was happening? I think your mama and I know a thing or two about you and Cooper Allen. I doubt you were really only getting coffee at Patty Cakes. Now, Mindy's worried we're about to have a repeat of your senior year summer, and we cannot have that." Mimi crosses her legs and I notice her cowboy boots. She has gone full rodeo princess this morning.

"Senior year summer wasn't so bad." That was the summer I spent with Cooper, the one when he finally noticed me. Then—bam—there was nothing but Cooper Allen until he left for football.

While I stayed in Mint Springs and watched my college dreams disappear.

My mother groans. "Not so bad? Hadley Jane, I don't know what planet you were on in August of that year, but the rest of us were on misery island dealing with you."

Mimi concurs, shaking her head vigorously. "You locked yourself in your room. You gave up Harvard, Hadley. *Harvard.*"

My grandmother knows almost nothing about my college hopes and dreams. She and Mama knew I was smart, and they were so proud of my grades and accomplishments, but they hadn't had a great grasp on the logistics of attending Harvard. I'd gotten in, and they had started thinking about the money, but hadn't realized chunks of it had started coming due much, much earlier. By the time I realized there was no way we could afford my Ivy League education, everyone already assumed I was going, Mama and Mimi included. The loss of Cooper had hit me hard, but that summer with him had at least given me something to take my mind off what I already knew—I wouldn't be going to Boston in September. I'd declined the offer of admission mid-summer.

But my family hadn't known that. They'd assumed I'd decided against college because I'd had my heart broken. No wonder Mindy hates Cooper. I'd hate him too if that was how things had happened.

"I didn't decide to stay home because of Cooper."

My mother's face clouds. "Yes you did. He left and you moped around, announced you weren't interested in college after all. We all thought you had lost your mind."

"I didn't go to Harvard because it was too expensive, Mama. I couldn't afford it."

"Of course *you* couldn't, Hadley, but we were working all that out." Mimi sounds so sure I almost wish I'd given her the chance to convince me of this years ago.

"I heard you talking—about selling the salon. We couldn't afford for me to go to Boston." I don't want to do anything to upset my mother or Mimi, but they need to know the real reason I stayed in Mint Springs.

"That wasn't a conversation for your ears, Hadley," my grandmother scolds. "And eavesdropping is rude."

"I didn't mean to overhear, but once I figured out y'all were talking about me…" I couldn't walk away from that, not at eighteen years old.

"We were working that out Hadley, and we could have come up with the money. Would have taken out loans if we needed to." My mother's slippered foot starts its rhythmic shaking again.

"I didn't want for everyone to go into debt for me, or to have to give up their own dreams." I glance around the salon. It's nowhere near ready to open, but it's one hundred percent my grandmother, and it's her life's work. I couldn't have let her sell it.

"Those were our decisions, Hadley. You mean to tell me you gave up your chance to have something you desperately wanted over something as silly as money?" The corners of Mimi's mouth turn down.

"Money we didn't have," I argue. "I did it to make sure you both didn't end up making a mistake."

"Seems to me the only mistake we've made is not forcing you to pack a bag and take the bus to Boston. You never got your degree." Mama's sigh is deep and sad in a way I hate to hear. In trying to make the best choice, I've disappointed her.

"I'm still getting it."

"Getting what?" Mimi asks.

"My degree. I've been working on it for a while now. I'm one class away from graduation." I can't hide the smile that overtakes my face.

"One class away?" Mimi's face lights up. "Why haven't you told us this?"

"I was nervous I wouldn't be able to do it." It's the first time I've said that out loud.

"Not able to? Hadley, you are a Crawford. You can do anything you set your mind to." My mother says it with so much conviction I actually believe it.

"That's why I've been spending so much time with Cooper. We're working on a project for this class. We'll graduate at the same time." I feel the slightest flutter at getting to include Cooper in my "we."

"So, you two are *studying*." Mimi winks again. "I guess we can have the graduation party and then the wedding."

"I wouldn't count on that." But the image of Cooper and me celebrating with our friends and families lodges in my brain and won't let go. It's not exactly my happy family fantasy, but it comes pretty close. *No, Hadley*, I remind myself, but I smile about it all day.

31

Cooper

"I'm not sure this is such a good idea."

"Why not?" Cade looks up from setting the table, still holding a fork in his hand. "People gotta eat."

"But people don't have to all eat *together*." I try to telegraph my apprehension to my youngest brother, but he keeps on putting forks and knives out like my world isn't about to tilt on its axis.

"You want to eat by yourself? You'd miss out on Sadie's chocolate cake. I already snuck a taste of the frosting so I can confirm it is delicious. Do those look alright?" Cade takes a step back from the table and scrutinizes his work.

"They look fine, Cade. No one cares if the forks are all completely straight."

"People care. If we're going to open a restaurant, you're going to have to start noticing details, Cooper." Cade adjusts one of the knives in front of him. "And we all want to make a good impression on your new girlfriend."

There it is.

"Hadley isn't my girlfriend, but I'll be sure to let her

know the place settings are all you." I frown at my grinning brother and consider how much trouble I'd get in if I gave him a shove over here by the dinner table.

"Not your girlfriend, huh?" Cade straightens a napkin. "That's not what I heard."

"Well, you heard wrong." I try to lean nonchalantly against the edge of the table. "Where exactly did you hear that anyway?"

"I'm not going to reveal my sources, but if I were you, I'd try to lock that down. Hadley's hot."

"Excuse me?" I rise up to my full height and lean toward my brother as menacingly as I'm allowed to here in Mae and Sadie's house.

"Whoa there, lover boy." Cade leans a hip against the table and smirks. Of course he's baiting me and, as usual, I'm unable to ignore it. "When's she getting here anyway?"

"She's coming with Lily. They've been out at the flea market picking out things for that big job Lily's got." And probably talking about all sorts of things I'd rather not have Lily know.

"Hope they get here soon. I'm ready for some fried chicken." Cade rubs his hands together. "You want to see if we can find Charlie and Chance and look at those plans again?"

"I don't think we have time." I'm kicking the can down the road here, but I need to put off the business discussions for a little longer. Hadley and I are almost ready for our presentation and then I'll be able to show my family what I'd like to add to the discussion.

"I'll be out on the porch, then. No use wasting the end of this beautiful day." Cade walks to the side door, letting himself out onto the screened-in porch just as Lily and Hadley come through the front door.

"Did you run Cade off?" Lily jokes.

"Hope so." I give Lily a peck on the cheek. "Y'all find what you needed?"

"That and more. Remind me not to bring Hadley with me next time. She convinced me to buy all sorts of crazy."

Hadley.

She's standing in front of me, smiling at me like we've been apart for days instead of hours. I can't keep the smile off my own face, even if it makes me look like a fool in front of my sister-in-law.

Lily clears her throat. "Why don't I go check on Cade?" she asks no one in particular as she leaves for the porch.

Hadley and I stand, staring at each other for a few beats. The ticking of my aunt Sadie's cuckoo clock matches my heartbeat.

"Come over here," I cajole.

"Absolutely not. I'm not about to let you paw all over me in your aunts' house."

I bark out a laugh before I sweep her up in my arms and press my lips to hers. I had planned on keeping things PG, but the dress she's wearing makes it difficult for me to keep my hands where they should be. If there was any way to whisk Hadley out of here and to somewhere more private, I'd do it.

"Oh, my." My aunt Mae's surprised voice interrupts my manhandling of Hadley. "Cooper Allen, not in my living room."

Hadley pulls away from me, covering her face with her hands. "I'm so sorry, Miss Mae," she whispers from between her fingers.

"Oh, Hadley, it's fine. I'm only teasing. I'm sure it's hard for the two of you to keep your hands to yourself now that you've given yourselves permission."

I reach for Hadley again but she swats my hands away. "Cooper, no," she scolds.

My aunt walks back into the kitchen laughing.

Not even the exaggerated pout I give her convinces Hadley to let me get back to kissing her. We're still having this standoff when the rest of my family comes tumbling into the house. Hadley fits right in with my brothers, and once we're all seated at the table and Mae's said grace, it's like she's been eating fried chicken with us forever. I position my chair closer to hers, and my brother Charlie gives me a raised eyebrow. I ignore him, keep the middle finger I consider brandishing for later, and let my left hand move over to Hadley's knee. She looks at me in surprise, but doesn't make me put my hand back where it belongs. I stroke the soft skin of her thigh and thank the universe for warm enough weather for Hadley to have put on a sundress.

"This chicken is delicious," Hadley tells my aunt in between bites. She does her groaning thing again, and my hand tightens on her leg.

"Mae's going to teach me how to make it." Lily pops another bite of macaroni and cheese in her mouth.

"And *she's* going to help us put in the garden." Sadie smiles over at Lily. My aunts are thrilled to finally have a girl in the family.

"When is this happening?" Hadley scoops some salad onto her fork.

"Next weekend. That's after Mother's Day. Which reminds me, you boys should all call your mama tomorrow. Although I'm sure y'all already knew that." Mae looks each of us in the eye. She knows how likely we are to forget something like Mother's Day. We're technically adults now, and not a one of us has much contact with either of our parents. A bad divorce will do that to you. Cade's the only one who manages to keep in touch with our mother, and Dad's the kind who'll be sure to show up for the good stuff but can't stomach the bad. Needless to say, he hasn't been around much lately. Our family's all right here, right now if you look for the people you can count on.

"It's early this year, but we never put the warm weather vegetables in before that." Sadie gives Mae a nod. "That's how we were taught to do it. After Mother's Day, or you risk losing your work."

"Can I help?" Hadley's question gets all my brothers looking up from their plates.

"Of course." Sadie's beaming again. "It'll be nice to have more helpers. These boys don't like to let us order them around."

"I'd love to see how you do it." Hadley slides her hand into mine under the table. "I could come over for chicken lessons and help with the garden before we put the finishing touches on our presentation."

My dinner sticks in my throat. I've been spending every free moment trying to catch up on the things I need to read to be able to finish my parts of the presentation. A few times I've been able to get Hadley to help me without her realizing she's doing it, but we're about to hit a point where it will be impossible to ignore.

"How's that coming?" Chance's making conversation, I doubt he's got any real interest in this, but Hadley answers like he's one of our classmates and our grade depends on it.

"It's going great. We cannot wait for y'all to see it."

"I thought this was an online class," Charlie pipes up from the other end of the table.

"It is, but we can do different things with the final presentation. There are points for creativity, and we need to make it as engaging as possible if we want to get an A." It's obvious Hadley will accept nothing less.

"Are we all invited?" Lily seems far too enthusiastic. This isn't going to be a party; it's most likely going to be my last stand.

"Yes!" Hadley's excitement means she's squeezing my hand harder than necessary. "We'd love for all of you to come."

As my family readily agrees, I realize it's too late for me to come up with an excuse. I wanted to show them what I could do.

Unfortunately, now they're going to see it.

32

Hadley

"Are we sure these are going to be okay? They're so little." I hold one of the seedlings closer to my face and look at the tomato plant's fuzzy leaves.

"It is still a little early. Mother's Day coming in early May can be tricky. But if it threatens to get too cold or there's a frost warning, we'll cover their little butts up." Mae wipes sweat from her brow. "But it's awfully hot today. Maybe there won't be any more cold nights."

I dig a hole in the soil like Mae showed me earlier. I'd showed up to the entire Allen family mucking around in the garden plot behind Sadie and Mae's house. Charlie was tilling up the ground and Cade was dumping new soil from the compost in with the old. Both of them were already shirtless at eight in the morning, streaked with dirt and sweating. I had hoped to see a sweaty, shirtless Cooper, but his job of hauling out all the flats of seedlings required much less visible chest. Once the heavy lifting was over, all the boys made themselves scarce.

"Did you grow all these from seed?" I'm still amazed at

all the things Sadie and Mae get up to. They're over here making homemade jam and biscuits, raising chickens, and growing food from nothing.

"Most of them." Sadie's stooped over her row of what will eventually be bell peppers, digging small holes for the seedlings in front of her. "Some of the supplies we get from Sullivan's. And Mae and I aren't as fastidious about saving our own seeds the way we used to be. That means buying a few packets here and there."

"I didn't see a greenhouse," I muse as I look around. I haven't had an opportunity to look around the Allen farm. In the summers I was usually just at the river, and that's a straight shot from here. I'd been to Sadie and Mae's house to have ice cream on the days when Cooper's grandfather would bring out the old ice cream maker. It had a hand crank and needed an entire bag of rock salt to make something we could have easily bought at the store. Of course, one bite made you change your mind about that, because nothing beats homemade ice cream on a hot day, especially when it takes an army to make it. Hand churned might look fancy on a package, but I know in real life it also can take the arm strength of several teenagers to make it happen.

I've spent plenty of time in the barn, too. Cooper and I used to sneak over to the hayloft when we wanted to be together without so many prying eyes. I'd go home with hay in my hair and a smile on my face.

"Mae and I grow seedlings in the house. We've got the basement all set up with lights and everything." Sadie gives me a nod.

I catch Lily's eye and she winks at me.

"I see you two looking at each other." Mae shakes a wrinkled finger at us. "We're strictly growing tomatoes down there. Don't think those boys of ours haven't already made every joke in the book."

Lily and I both laugh, and Sadie and Mae join in. The idea of the two of them growing what Mae will later call "wacky tobacky" has us all giggling. Inside though, I'm smiling just as big at the fact that Mae called Cooper and his brothers "their boys." There's a lot of love over here at the Allen farm, and my heart swells a little at getting to be a part of it.

After we wash all the dirt off, Sadie and Mae give me and Lily a chicken lesson. It's nearly as sweaty as gardening, frying a chicken, but by the end of the afternoon, I think I've got the hang of it.

"Now don't go around telling people about the brine," Mae cautions, her gray curls bobbing.

"Well, they can tell people there's a *brine*, but don't tell anyone the *ingredients*," Sadie chimes in, wiping flour from her hands onto the front of her apron. "The process—you can say things about it—but be a little...vague."

"This is why you can never trust the recipes on our website if they came from Sadie and Mae." Lily gives them a *tsk tsk*. "Keeping people from being able to have something as delicious as this chicken..." She takes another bite.

"We teach it to *family*, Lily. Our recipes are for you and Hadley, not all the riff-raff." Mae purses her lips. "You have to *earn* them."

My heart nearly bursts, and my eyes well with tears. I'm not family—not really—and I'm not sure what I did to be given that honor. I pretend to be very interested in my three bean salad, sure everyone can see how desperate I am for Mae's words to be true.

This is not me protecting my heart. Not at all.

One by one, the boys trickle in. Chance, Charlie, and

Cade all sample our attempt at fried chicken and give it the muted praise it deserves, considering we all know who the reigning fried chicken queens of the Allen family are and will be for a while yet. But Cooper never comes in for lunch. I start to ask, but get self-conscious. I don't want everyone to think he's been on my mind all day, even if he has.

As we finish the dishes, Mae hands me a plate piled high with all the fixings from lunch, wrapped tight in cling film. "Here, you go on and take a plate to Cooper. He's got to be starving by now. One of the boys can run you out to his house to deliver it."

"Cooper's house?" I've heard talk of Cooper building a house, but he's never said anything about it to me. It's another one of those things I'm not supposed to have any interest in, but I'm insanely curious about.

"Oh!" Lily lights up. "You haven't seen it, have you? Chance can take you out there. I cannot wait to hear what you think of it." She runs off to get her husband to be my chauffeur.

"Thank you both, for letting me help today." I'm surprisingly bashful now, alone with Mae and Sadie. I feel like a teenager again, here in their house trying to make a good impression—something I'm sure I didn't always do when I was seventeen.

"We were glad to have you," Sadie crows as she wraps her arms around me. I work hard not to fumble the plate of Cooper's chicken.

"Yes, yes, any time. We need more ladies out here." Mae pats my arm, her weathered hand surprisingly soft against my skin. "Now go on and get that plate to your boy before he gnaws off his hand."

I nearly skip to Chance's truck, the good feelings from the house following me the entire way.

"You ready to see this?" Chance gives me a grin.

"I think so." I try to keep the plate steady as we bounce long the gravel road. "Should I be worried or something?"

"No." Chance shakes his blond head. "I think you're going to be pleasantly surprised."

Pleasantly surprised doesn't begin to cover how I feel once we make it to the top of the rise, where Cooper's house is under construction. What looks like the entire world is spread out in front of us. The late afternoon sun is still high enough in the sky for me to need to shield my eyes with my hand, but I can clearly make out the frame of a pretty good-sized house, and Cooper standing in what will eventually be the front yard. It's breathtaking, and it's not even finished yet.

Chance puts the truck in park, but he doesn't get out. Instead, he rolls down the window and yells to his brother, "Brought you some lunch! And a pretty girl!"

I roll my eyes but appreciate Chance's compliment. "Thanks for the ride." I open my door and slide out into the sunshine.

Cooper's over to meet me in two seconds flat. He's obviously been working—sawdust clings to his hair and his arms—but I don't mind any of that when he lowers his face to mine and gives me the world's sweetest kiss. "Is that fried chicken?" he asks, reaching for the plate.

"That *I* made," I boast, puffing up more than I should, considering the amount of help I had. "Mae made you a plate. Thought you were out here dying of starvation."

"Not dead yet, but pretty close." Cooper's grin is wide enough to take up his entire face.

"This is really beautiful." I give the space around me another look. I had pictured some kind of cabin in the woods, but this is a house—a real house. The kind you put a family in, the kind you settle in forever.

"Wait until you see the inside." Cooper excitedly takes my hand, pulling me toward the front porch.

"Aren't you going to eat?" I laugh, letting him guide me closer to the house.

"That can wait, dazzling you with Casa Cooper cannot." He gives me another quick kiss and then leads me up the steps and through the front door.

33

Cooper

It's surreal to be leading Hadley up the steps and into my house. I've pictured her here a million times, but that's always been a fantasy. This moment is as real as it gets: her hand in mine and nothing to stop me from pulling her through the front door. I leave the plate of Hadley's fried chicken on one of the sawhorse tables in the front hallway. The place is still definitely a work in progress. It's all framed up, and we've got the roof on, and while it's obvious it's a house, it doesn't have any of the final touches I'm planning. Hell, it doesn't even have any of the drywall hung yet.

Still, Hadley coos like I've brought her inside a mansion, and her enthusiasm only builds as we traipse through the rooms.

"Four bedrooms?" Hadley tilts her head. "That's more than I would have thought you'd want."

"It's too big, probably, but I can use one room as an office." I don't confess how I've thought about putting kids in those bedrooms, filling this house with little people and letting them run wild in the woods next door. Hadley doesn't need to know about those dreams.

The kitchen nearly makes her faint.

"Are you kidding me?" Hadley's eyes bulge out of her head. "And the view from in here!" She looks out the windows in the breakfast nook. "I've never noticed how pretty those mountains are."

"I tried to position the house so that every room's got a great view." It's something I'm proud of, even if no one notices but me. Hadley notices, though, and that makes my chest hurt a little in a way I haven't felt in a long while.

"Show me more," Hadley demands and we go through the entire thing, room by room. I point out all the things I'm going to do to make the house special—the finishes and trim ideas, the built-in shelves, the appliance pantry Mae told me was "divine." When I'm finally done and we're back on the porch, I'm high on the way Hadley's loved everything I've got planned.

"I've never been out here, I don't think." Hadley scans the land around the house.

"Nobody really comes out here but me." I shrug. "It's got a special place in my heart."

This has Hadley's interest. "And why's that? You deflower someone particularly memorable up here on this hill?"

I laugh, but it isn't genuine. I hate that Hadley thinks I'd pick a spot to build my forever home on because of some girl, especially since only one girl would have inspired that kind of devotion. "If I had done that, I'd be living in the barn."

The tiniest bit of pink spreads across Hadley's cheeks. "Why's it special then?"

"I'll show you." I give her my hand again and she takes it, ready to let me lead her wherever. I take her down to the edge of the pine trees, filling my lungs with the smell of the forest mixed with Hadley's perfume. When I start to take her into the woods, she hesitates, pulling back a bit.

"Why do I feel like Little Red Riding Hood right now?"

"I'm not the Big Bad Wolf, Hadley. Trust me." It's unfair, and I know it. Hadley shouldn't be trusting me at all after the way I've treated her—not today, not yesterday, not tomorrow—but I want her to with a fierceness I can't control. I want it almost as much as I want her forgiveness. Almost as much as I want her love, even if I don't deserve it.

She lets the tug of my hand pull her closer to me, almost flat against my chest. She's shorter than I'm used to, since for once she had the good sense to wear sneakers. I had expected her to show up for a day of gardening in some kind of high-heeled sandal. That would have been classic Hadley. Instead, she's in shorts and a T-shirt, her long blonde hair in a ponytail and sporting some canvas sneakers that look like they've never been worn before.

Hadley moves closer, and I wrap my arms around her. I put a kiss on the top of her head. "We're only going a little ways in."

We move between the trees on the well-worn path that takes us to the clearing where the still used to sit. It's a round opening in the woods where none should be, and I hear Hadley take in a sharp breath once we're in the middle. She tilts her head and looks at me, waiting for me to explain.

"Allens used to make moonshine right here during prohibition."

Hadley's wide eyes take in the space. "There was a still *here*? How do you know that?"

"My grandpa told me, years ago. Eddie knows the family recipe, too."

"We *have* to make it, then." Hadley's determined voice

echoes off the tall trees. "It'll be the first thing we make, one of the things we sell while we wait for our own whiskey to age."

"Moonshine? I thought we were going to source the first batches from MGP. That's what everyone does starting out." We'd heard over and over again on the tours about how new places bought their first few batches of whiskey from a supplier in Indiana. Aging takes years and that way you didn't have to wait. Some brands still used purchased whiskey to blend with their own and Hadley and I'd incorporated purchased whiskey into our own distillery plan from the start.

"We're going to make moonshine. *Allen* moonshine. That's the story, Cooper. You're not some Johnny-come-lately to this thing; it's in your family's history. Moonshine's a perfectly respectable beginning for this distillery. We can buy all the whiskey from Indiana we want, but that's not going to have the story this will." She turns in a slow circle, and I can't take my eyes off her. She's learned so much about distilling and whiskey, gotten so good at the business side of things. If this distillery ever becomes more than a thought in my head, I don't know how I'll make it successful without Hadley.

There is no way I can keep from walking from my spot to the one in front of Hadley. No way I can keep my hands from cupping her face or keep from kissing her. I pour all the things I'm feeling right now into that kiss, hoping she can feel how much I love everything about her—the way she makes me feel, the way she makes me feel about myself. I'm considering laying her down right here on the pine needles when my stomach growls.

Hadley's laugh fills the clearing. "Time to feed you, Cooper Allen."

∼

We sit on the front porch and share the plate of food Hadley brought me. Although "share" isn't the right word, exactly, because while I'm inhaling everything, she's only taking little nibbles.

"Aren't you hungry?" I ask through a mouth full of fried chicken.

"I ate more than I should have earlier. We had to taste test everything, you know." Hadley pats her belly but still sneaks another sliver of chicken. "How do you think it turned out?"

"*Terrible*. I can hardly stand to eat it." I tear another bite of meat off the leg I'm munching on. "You should probably try again tomorrow."

"Don't tease. I know it isn't up to Mae and Sadie standards, but it's good, right?"

"It's better than good. And my aunts have decades of practice feeding hungry Allens. There's no way to compete with them. You should have seen the way they used to feed us when we were working. The biggest lunch you can imagine, and they'd do it every day of the summer." I smile thinking about those days. They were some of the most carefree I'd ever had and maybe ever will. Working with my grandpa made me feel useful, competent. Summers were never long enough to completely erase the bad feelings from the school year before, but they helped. I always dreaded August, because it meant leaving Georgia and going back to a life of missed assignments and disappointing grades back in Nashville.

"I can imagine Sadie and Mae doing that with smiles on their faces. They love you and your brothers so much it almost hurts to watch." Hadley's wistful, and I reach out to hold her hand.

"They don't have kids of their own. I guess that's why they're so attached."

"I think it's more than that. My mama loves me—my grandmother too. And Mindy loves me in her own way, even if it is infuriating sometimes. But Sadie and Mae...there's something so fierce about the way they love you, the way they claim you boys."

I think about that, remembering all the times as a teenager that my brothers and I descended on the farm and threw everything into chaos. But my grandpa always seemed to love it, Mae and Sadie too, even if we were a handful. We were lucky to have that.

"Look at that. Cooper, you have been holding out one me."

I'm not sure exactly what Hadley's talking about until I look out over the hill. The sun's setting, and tonight it's even more beautiful than usual. The pinks and purples and oranges are melting behind the mountain, spreading out like a painting.

"Happens every night," I brag. "But his one's exceptional. Must be the company." I wipe my hands and mouth on the napkin Mae's tucked under the plate.

"Must be." She gives me a shy smile. "You know what you need out here? A porch swing. Right over there." She points to the edge of the porch.

"I was thinking of putting some rocking chairs out here, but that would work too." I imagine the swing hanging at the end on the porch, and Hadley and I snuggled up in it to watch the sunset. Like tonight, but more permanent. She'd be mine, and we could have nights like this any time we wanted. I reach for her and she comes, letting me pull her close.

Hadley hums contentedly as we kiss, her body flush against mine. "See? We could be doing this in a *swing*."

I laugh, my mouth still pressed against the skin of her collarbone. "I'll get one for you."

"You'd better," she breathes into the top of my head, her fingers sliding through my hair. Then there's no more talking as we surrender to each other.

Even though no one's likely to come out here, I still stand up and hoist Hadley into my arms. The house isn't really much of a house yet, and it'll be a long while before it'll be a home, but tonight that's what it feels like as I carry her through the front door and bring her into the room that will eventually be my bedroom.

I ease Hadley down to the floor, fully aware this isn't the most comfortable spot we could choose. But I've got a sleeping bag and some quilts from the last time I spent the night out here, before we put on the roof when you could see the stars through the rafters.

"Bringing a girl back to your room already?" Hadley jokes, although the heat in her voice keeps me from laughing.

"Too soon?" I make sure to position her on the stack of quilts. "No bed in here yet."

Hadley answers me with a long lingering kiss, and we set to work christening my new bedroom.

Hadley

Maybe I'm a fool for letting Cooper bring me back to his bedroom. In truth, it's barely a room right now—the floor's plywood subflooring and we're already engulfed in darkness since the sun's set. I won't be the only woman to be in this bedroom with Cooper, if the past's any indication, but I couldn't resist the idea of being the first. Would I like to think I might be the last? Sure, I won't lie. But I'm trying to keep expectations low, even if in my heart I know I'm failing miserably.

I let Cooper's hands roam where they will, loving the feel of his touch. The calluses that scrape over my skin are a testament to the things he's building here—both literally and figuratively. I'm surrounded by his handiwork as his mouth ravages mine. He pulls my T-shirt over my head and tosses it behind him, lowering his head to my chest. He unhooks my bra as his tongue moves down the groove between my breasts. I tilt my head back to bare myself even more to him, and Cooper murmurs appreciatively. His fingers move to the button of my shorts, not wasting any time.

In the dark I need to rely on feel. Even though my eyes have adjusted, we're still only shadows. I grip Cooper's arms as his fingers dip low, trying to kick off my shoes at the same time. I fumble around, pulling on his T-shirt but not wanting to thwart anything his hands might be planning for me. The quilts underneath me keep the plywood from biting into my back, but this location's not the most comfortable for what's happening. That certainly doesn't stop either one of us—it barely slows us down.

Cooper's laughing as he pulls his shirt off and gives it a toss. I take this opportunity to slide out of my shorts. We're as impatient as we used to be in the hayloft, rolling around on these blankets like teenagers. And it feels the way it used to—easy, free—so I let those feelings keep washing over me even as my brain tries to remind me these moments are fleeting.

"Hadley." He says my name like a prayer, like a whispered promise, and I feel my heart open another tiny crack. Cooper's working his way in there, bit by little bit, and there's nothing I can do to stop it. Not that I would; I'm a fool for starting this up again, but I've still got my foot on the gas even if I know there might be danger up ahead. I lie back and watch as Cooper slides quickly out of his jeans, shucking his boxers in the same movement. Then he's back hovering over me and handing me the condom packet.

I tear the foil open and use safe sex as an excuse to run my hands all over him. Cooper groans and returns the favor by sliding his fingers down between my legs. He groans again when he realizes how wet I am. He raises up and positions himself between my legs, his eyes glittering in the darkness.

"Please," I beg, and he doesn't wait another second; he slides in, filling me. I'm vaguely aware of Cooper trying to keep from crushing me against the unforgiving surface of the floor, but that barely registers. We could be lying on a bed of nails, and I still wouldn't ask Cooper to stop. I rise up to meet him on every stroke, wanting more. There will never be enough of this to satisfy me, not in a million years, and there'll never be another man who makes me feel as desperate as Cooper does. I'm sure of it.

I wrap my legs around Cooper's waist and pull him closer. The change in angle has us both panting, racing for the finish line. I can feel my orgasm building, and I dig my fingers into Cooper's back, clawing at him. I'm arching up against him, shaking with pleasure when he stiffens against me, calling out my name for the entire world to hear.

Later we rest, legs tangled together, in the pile of quilts. Cooper keeps me positioned on top of him, taking most of the brunt of the floor. His fingertips trace along my back, stopping on my shoulder blades.

"Did you get scratched up?"

I wince when his finger finds the places where the quilts weren't enough protection. "A little."

"I'm sorry, baby. I should have noticed. We could have changed positions or something. We could have stopped." The concern in Cooper's voice is a comfort and soothes the scrapes more than any salve ever could.

"It'll be fine," I whisper against his chest.

I hope I'm right.

34

Cooper

"What if we set up over here?" Hadley points to the back of the room. "If we use the back, we don't have to do the whole room, just what's visible on camera."

"That sounds good." I don't lift my eyes from the papers in front of me.

"We can get some flowers, use those barrel tables over here... Ohhh, what about moving that neon sign? Is it hard to move, do you think? Or is that not the right vibe? Are you sure we can't ask Lily to help with this? She'd have this all sorted out in five minutes, and she's got connections we could use for other things we want."

"Um hum."

"'Um hum' meaning I *can* call Lily? Are you even listening?"

I look up to see an angry Hadley with her hands on her hips. Uh oh.

"I'm listening. You said we should just use the back." At least that's what I hope Hadley said. I've been focused on trying to read some of the class material I've fallen behind on, and it is not going well. Today's the last real day to iron out the details of our presentation here at Eddie's, so I'm trying to multi-task, another thing I already know I'm terrible at doing.

"And what did I say after that?"

I freeze, my brain whirring at a million miles a second. I'm losing the battle here, and I've never been great at the war. Hadley's sure to figure out how much I have left to do, and I'm not sure I can catch up. Being a terrible listener is the least of my worries.

"Did you say I'm the most amazing man you've ever met and you're really hoping I can do that thing I did this morning again, possibly later today?" I waggle my eyebrows at her, hoping that sounds dickish enough to distract her but not dickish enough to make her madder than she's already threatening to be.

"Cooper! We don't have time for that," Hadley protests, but she smiles and blushes enough to let me know I've done what I set out to do. "But I might be able to fit you in later if you concentrate now."

"Ah, you're bribing me." I put the papers down and move to pull Hadley into my arms.

"Seriously, Cooper." She gives me her sternest face. "We have to get this work done today. To-day."

"I think we have time for one kiss, don't you? Maybe two?" I press my lips to hers, but Hadley doesn't budge. She keeps her mouth tight, her lips unyielding against mine. "Really?" I laugh. "Such a task master."

"What in the world are you doing to that poor girl?" Eddie chooses that moment to come back from checking the tanks. "If that's how you've been going about it, I'm not surprised you've been single for so long, Cooper."

"I'm trying to distract Hadley, but it's not working," I tell him, as Hadley squirms against me.

"Well, I can see why. Are you tryin' to kiss her or twist her into a pretzel? Let the poor girl go." Eddie shakes his head.

I give Hadley a smacking kiss on the cheek before I release her. "How's our batch looking back there?"

"Coming along nicely," Eddie confirms. "I think the Allen moonshine is going to be delicious. Cooper's a natural. I always said he had a feel for it, and I think it really shows."

"And it'll be ready in time for our presentation?" Hadley's eager voice reminds me why we're all here. The dreaded presentation, currently only a few days away.

"Yes, Miss Hadley. Your moonshine'll be ready. Y'all need to hurry up on the labels, though, if you want the bottles to look professional." Eddie gives his beard a scratch. "Y'all decide on a name?"

"Not yet. We have a difference of opinion." Hadley shoots me a look.

"Can't we just call it Allen Moonshine?" I look hopefully at Eddie.

"You know we can't. If it's going to be the first thing we sell, it needs to have a name as special as the product." Hadley cocks one hip and dares me to contradict her.

"Your girl's right. You can't half-ass this, Cooper, and you shouldn't want to." Eddie gives Hadley a nod. "Anything I can help you with out here?"

"Yes! I have a question about the neon sign. Can we move it here?" Hadley gestures toward the back wall.

"I guess. It's heavy, though." Eddie looks at me and raises an eyebrow.

"We can do it together," I volunteer. "While we do that,

can I get you to read this out loud? That way I can do two things at once."

"Smart," Hadley says, reaching for the papers I've left on the counter and never suspecting how not smart I really am. "Are you rereading all of these?" She flips through the articles from earlier in the semester. The ones I've never actually finished reading.

"Thought I should review them. See if there's anything in those we need to think about for the presentation." I leave out all the missing assignments I really need them for.

"That's a good idea." Hadley sits on one of the bar stools. "I'll read while you two move that sign."

"Sounds like a good trade," Eddie says, muttering "for Cooper" under his breath. I pretend not to hear him as we lift the giant neon sign and shuffle our way across the warehouse.

As we work, Hadley's voice carries through the space, telling us all about the importance of digital marketing. I avoid looking at Eddie. He knows all about my difficulties with reading. He'd never say anything to anyone, but he's more than aware of the white lie I've just told Hadley.

"This where you want it?"

"That's perfect. Eddie, are you okay with it staying here for a few days?" Hadley comes over to give the sign a closer inspection.

"I'm fine with that. Looks pretty good here, actually. Maybe I'll leave it here permanently." Eddie stands beside Hadley, his head tilt mirroring hers.

"You mean you might keep it somewhere people might actually see it?" I fake a gasp.

"Well, now that you two have done the work, I can see how the space might look all fixed up. It is *inspiring* me, Cooper." Eddie's sarcasm isn't lost on me even if I know there's a grain of truth in there. The place is looking great, like an actual business, and Eddie has Hadley to thank for that. I can take a little of the credit, but it's her work that's making the difference.

"I'd be happy to help with the rest of the place," Hadley tells him, already getting excited. "I have some ideas for the bar area I think you're really going to like. And I'm thinking about getting some potted plants and flowers for the day of the presentation. We could do that for the front too."

"Slow down, slow down," Eddie cautions. "One thing at a time. Why don't y'all take a break and come in the back to show Hadley how your product's doing?"

Hadley follows along behind him, and I reluctantly join them. I've been checking on this moonshine religiously since we started on the batch. It doesn't have to be perfect—but it needs to be pretty damn close to convince anyone this will be a good idea. Already Charlie and Cade have big plans for their restaurant. I want my liquor to be something that's an easy sell. It isn't whiskey, but they're close cousins, and I'm hoping the business plan will sell them on the idea as much as the moonshine samples we're planning on giving out.

"Come on, Cooper," Hadley yells over her shoulder. "We don't have all day."

She's right about that. And after this I've got farm chores and more school work. I'll be up half the night doing my damndest to keep my head above water. The quicker we finish here, the better.

35

Hadley

If there has ever been a more perfect late spring day, I don't think I've ever seen it. Although lately almost every day seems nearly perfect. It could be the gorgeous weather that shows no sign of stopping, or the fact that I'm days away from really finishing college, but it's most likely the result of the man sitting next to me, dangling one hand out the open truck window. Cooper's got on a pair of ridiculous sunglasses, and he grins when he catches me staring at him.

"What?"

"Nothing, just admiring your profile." I turn back toward the windshield and stifle a giggle.

"It's the glasses, right? They really do make this outfit." He gestures down the length of his body. He's still dressed in some exceptionally filthy blue jeans and a T-shirt that's seen better days. We're off to Sullivan's Nursery to make sure the plants and flowers I want to spruce up Eddie's will be available when we need them so clothes fresh from farm work won't be out of place. I could have taken care of this myself, but Cooper insisted on coming. As we get closer to the end of the semester, he's gotten busier and busier. With less time to spend together, I was thrilled he'd wanted to come with me. If this is all I can get for the next few days, I'll happily take it.

"I am in awe of those glasses."

"Chance says they make me look like a TV housewife, but I think that's his jealousy talking." Cooper slides the glasses down the bridge of his nose and looks at me over the top of the lenses. "They make me even more irresistible, don't they?"

"Oh, they make you something, alright."

"Like a supermodel? Not everyone can pull this look off, you know." He slides the shades back up.

"Oh, believe me, I know." I'm only half joking. Ridiculous sunglasses aside, there are many things only Cooper Allen can pull off.

When we're parked in the gravel lot, I wait for Cooper to come around and open my door. You wouldn't think he'd have strong feelings about something like that, but I've found one thing Cooper likes to do is take care of me. And I do wear the kinds of shoes that make getting in and out of a pickup truck a little difficult. He reaches for my hand to help me out and doesn't let go. Walking hand in hand with Cooper still gives me a little thrill. By now it's no secret we're together, but I still love being able to make it clear to whomever might be looking. I know it's prideful to be showing off like that, but I can't seem to help myself.

Cooper nods to everyone we pass, exchanging hellos. By the time we get to the register, it feels like we've seen half the population of Mint Springs. Trey Sullivan waves excitedly from the other side of the counter.

"Well, look who's here," Cooper calls out. "Didn't think you'd be around until summertime."

"I'm up for the weekend. It's Dad's birthday. I usually can't come much during the season, but this is an exception." Trey is the carbon copy of his father—red hair, blue eyes, and a talent for baseball that might have him following in his dad's footsteps and playing in the major leagues.

"And he's got you workin'?" Cooper shakes his head. "How's school? This your last year?" Cooper asks, and Trey shakes his head.

"I'm a junior. One more year after this." He cuts his eyes to the floor. "Provided I pass everything."

"No shame in summer school," Cooper says and raises his fist for Trey to bump his only slightly smaller one against. "How's your season going?"

At this Trey lights up and starts rambling off baseball stats that have Cooper getting excited and me getting bored. "I'm going to look for Laney," I call out to them, waving as I move away from them.

I find Trey's almost-stepmother back in her painting studio. It's technically a shed behind the nursery, but there really is something magical about the space. Laney's contorted over a canvas she's got on the floor, putting huge swaths of paint over it. She's a local girl, but spent years in New York. She's had gallery shows and write-ups in the *New York Times*, but now she's back in Mint Springs, madly in love with her high school sweetheart again. I know it shouldn't give me as much hope as it does, but it's hard not to let Laney's seemingly perfect life give me hope for a happily ever after of my own.

"Hadley!" Laney calls out when she sees me. "Come and give me your opinion."

I walk closer to the canvas. "I'm not sure you want my opinion when it comes to art, Laney."

"Why not? You're an artist. I've seen what you can do

with even the worst sort of canvas over at the salon." Laney gives me a wink and pats her ponytail. "I'm trying something a little bold, but I'm not sure if it's too much. What do you think?"

I look at the wide slashes of color. They're layered over one of Laney's more traditional paintings. It almost looks like the old painting's been destroyed—vandalized—and I'm not sure if I hate it or love it. "It's a little...violent, don't you think? Will people think you've ruined the painting underneath?"

"Maybe. But maybe they'll think I've liberated it." Laney dusts her hands off on the front of her coveralls. "What brings you out here today?"

"Cooper and I need to get some plants and order some flowers. We're doing a little browsing."

"You and Cooper? Well, that's interesting." Laney's mouth quirks up into a little half grin. "Do you need my help?"

"No, I think Trey can probably take care of it. He's talking to Cooper now. They're dissecting everything baseball." I peer around the corner to look at them. Cooper's animatedly telling Trey something, his hands flying around. He's got those sunglasses perched on the top of his head, and the smile on his face forces one onto my face to match.

"Those two are peas in a pod," Laney says, laughing. "It's nice that Cooper takes the time to talk to Trey. It helps him feel less alone, I think."

"What do you mean?" I look at Laney and her brow furrows.

"Cooper had some of the same challenges Trey's having. With school, you know." Laney looks at me like I'm an idiot.

"No, I don't know." I take another look at Cooper and a million puzzle pieces fall into place.

"Oh...it's probably nothing. And it's not my place to say. Forget I said anything." Laney waves her hand like she can wish the whole conversation away.

But now the wheels are turning in my head—the requests for me to read out loud, the way he doesn't want to share assignments. He'd said he didn't want to have it look like we were working together, but what if he didn't want to show me his work? All the things I've thought of as entitlement or laziness now butt up against a new set of parameters. I try to think back to times he's needed to write something down, or if I've ever seen Cooper read a book for fun. I come up empty.

"But Trey has dyslexia. Does Cooper have dyslexia?" I look at Laney and then back toward the man who I thought I was getting to know so well.

"I don't honestly know, Hadley. I assumed.... I've really put my foot in it, I think." She does that floppy thing with her hands, shaking them out. "Why don't we go and get you set up for flowers?"

"Has Cooper told you he has a learning disability?"

"The preferred terminology is learning *challenge*, and, no, he hasn't. I just assumed from everything I've heard. And the way he relates to Trey. I'm sorry. I've overstepped." She herds me back to the main nursery building, chattering all the while about how lovely the peonies are right now. I'm on autopilot, choosing the things I want to help decorate Eddie's distillery.

"Do you want to pick up day before or day of?" Laney asks, and I'm so deep in my own world I barely hear her.

"Day before." Cooper's next to me, his hand brushing against the small of my back. "I'll come and get them." He turns toward me. "That's better, right? Then we can be set up the night before. Or do you want them same day? Your call." He smiles, and I reflexively smile back.

"No, day before is probably safer." I let Cooper take care of the rest of the order, hardly even helping to pick out the bigger potted plants I'd said I wanted to help fill the space.

"You okay?" Cooper asks as he loads my purchases in the back of the truck. "I promise I'll drive slow enough to keep all the leaves on these things, if that's what you're worried about."

"I'm a little tired I think," I lie. "Do you think you can drop me off at my place? I might try to take a nap."

"You want company?" Cooper's voice is husky. He's hoping "nap" is a euphemism.

"No, thanks." I reach for his hand and give it a squeeze. He keeps a tight grip on me and raises my hand to his lips.

"I'll take these to Eddie's and you rest, then. Can't have you comin' down with anything right before our big day." Cooper's eyes crinkle at the edges, a look of concern on his face. He leans over to kiss me. "It's all coming together, Hadley."

When he drops me off, he's all smiles again, opening my door and making sure I'm safely inside before he drives off again. "Enjoy your nap," he calls out before I shut the door.

But I don't even try to rest. Instead, I pull out my laptop and fire up the search engine.

36

Hadley

I'm sitting at the kitchen table when Cooper lets himself into my apartment. "Hadley? I used the key. Hope that's okay. Are you decent?" He comes into the room and looks disappointed when he sees I'm dressed. "I was hoping you weren't decent."

I want to smile, but the best I can manage is a little shrug. I'm still in my pajamas from the night before, although I haven't done much sleeping.

"Are you still not feeling great? I brought my computer, but we don't have to do work. I'm feeling pretty confident with what we have so far, and we've got four more days. If you need a break, we could play hooky." He settles himself into the chair across from me and lifts my feet into his lap. "We could...go and get pie at Patty Cakes. Or we could grab a quilt and drive down to the river. You want to have a picnic? What time do you need to be at the salon?" He rubs my feet as he talks, thinking of all the ways for us to wile away the day together.

"Why didn't you tell me?"

"Tell you what?" He's still got that handsome smile on his face, still unaware of what I know.

"About your learning disability?"

His fingers stop moving. "My what?"

"The dyslexia, Cooper. Why didn't you tell me about that? Did you not trust me enough?" My voice gets unusually high.

"I don't have any idea what you're talking about." Cooper stares at me in confusion. "Why would you think I have dys —whatever you said."

"You know what I said, Cooper. I don't know why I didn't see it before—the way you want me to read the articles to you all the time, the way you use the dictation on your phone for lists. Those are ways to circumvent the problems you have with reading and writing. I looked all of it up. You didn't have to be sneaky about it. I would have understood." I think I might cry, but I'm not sure if it's because Cooper's been lying to me or because the lie is so ridiculous.

"Hadley, I've never said I was a genius. You know I've never been an A student." Cooper's volume starts to increase. "You think I like you knowing all the answers all the time?"

"I'm not...I don't always know the answers."

"Well, you seem to know all the answers when it comes to this." Cooper stands. "I'm not the smartest guy in the room. You think I don't know that? If you wanted a reason to call things off you should have just said. You don't have to act like you've caught me in some lie." He spits the last part out, and I wince.

"I want you to be honest, that's all." I can't believe Cooper's denying he's been keeping this from me.

"I have been, Hadley. As much as I could be."

"As much as you could be? What does that mean?" My head aches from all this back and forth.

"It doesn't mean anything. Jesus, Hadley, nothing I say is good enough, and you're twisting my words. I can't win." Cooper's moving toward the door before I have a chance to say anything more.

"Are you leaving?" I jump to my feet. "You're walking out? We're not even going to talk about this?"

"What is there to talk about? You think you've cracked the code on why I'm not the great American novelist, right? You've figured out I'm an idiot. Well, congratulations. Sorry I'm not going to stick around so you can test out any of your brilliant theories on me." Cooper stomps through the living room and back out the front door, slamming it behind him.

"Thank you so much for comin' over here. I wouldn't have called you, but we don't know what else to do. It's an *emergency*." My sister's voice cuts through the fog in my brain. "She's back here."

"Thank the Lord!" my mother yells as Lily takes one of the seats at the break room table. "I've got clients. *She's* got clients. See if you can figure out what's wrong with her."

I don't look at Lily, just keep turning over this morning's events in my head. My conversation with Cooper went off the rails in spectacular fashion, but there's still a part I can't wrap my head around. Now I'm sitting in this uncomfortable chair, a cold cup of coffee in front of me, and my entire family on red alert.

"She's been sitting like that for more than an hour. Not talkin' or anything. Staring straight ahead like that. Do you think she's had a stroke?" Mimi comes over to look at me.

"We've had to reschedule two appointments already. Hadley, honey, what's wrong?"

"Hadley?" Lily gives my arm a poke. "What's going on?"

"I think I messed something up."

"She speaks! Finally! Now do you think you could possibly get your ass up and start Bitsy Miller's perm? She's been waiting fifteen minutes. Claims you're the only one she trusts to do it." My sister beckons for me to move from my seat.

"Give us a minute, Mindy," Lily requests, still regarding me with a mix of apprehension and curiosity. Once Mindy returns to work, huffing and puffing like she's having an asthma attack, Lily turns toward me. "What did you mess up?"

"Things with Cooper." It's the first time I've said it out loud, but I know it's true. Cooper is furious with me. I had thought it should be me all full of rage and fury, but instead I'm still putting the pieces together.

"I'm sure that's not right. Did y'all have a fight?" Lily's big brown eyes blink at me. Ah, for things to be so easy.

"I accused him of something," I explain.

"Oh? What did he do?" Lily sounds genuinely disappointed. "Hopefully nothing too awful. He's not a saint, but I was hoping he wasn't...you know."

"A dog?" I offer.

My sister's all over that in a flash. "A dog? Who? Cooper? Hadley, I hate to say I told you so, but—"

"Everybody knows you don't hate it. Shut up, Mindy." I wave her away, and she stomps off again. Unfortunately, her chair's closest to the break room so I know she'll be back to offer her comments on anything else I say. "I thought he was keeping something from me."

"Well, was he?" Lily's not exactly a neutral party here.

Cooper is her brother-in-law, and that might trump lifelong best friend, but I think she'll be able to shed some light on what's happened.

"He didn't tell me about his learning disability. Sorry, *challenge.*"

"His what?" Lily cocks her head to the side.

"His dyslexia. I told him I knew and he could have trusted me enough to tell me." There. I've laid it all out.

"Cooper doesn't have dyslexia." Lily's words poke a little hole through the fog. "Or if he does, this is the first I'm hearing about it."

"He obviously has dyslexia, Lily. I did all this research. All the classic signs are there." I argue my case, even though I have a terrible feeling about where this is going.

"He's never been an academic all-star. You know that. But I've never heard anything about him having a learning challenge. I always assumed he wasn't interested in school —that it wasn't his thing." Lily shrugs. "I think their parents always thought Cooper was a little lazy."

"He's not lazy!" I shout and both my mama and Mimi come scooting into the room.

"Girls," my mother angrily whispers. "We have clients in the next room. And Cooper's not lazy. No one really thinks that, Hadley. Calm down."

"Can I get a little privacy?" I look from my mother to my grandmother.

"Not if you're sitting in here you can't. You should know that." Mimi shakes her head. "This is about boy trouble? I thought you'd lost your marbles. There's no reason for a come apart over a little misunderstanding."

"I think maybe we had more than a misunderstanding." I think back to the moments before Cooper stormed out of my apartment. "I told him he has a learning disability and then accused him of lying to me about it."

"Cooper has a learning disability? What does that mean?" Mimi turns to look at Mama like *she* has the answers.

"The thing is, I don't think Cooper does have a learning disability." I look at Lily. "Right? He doesn't."

"He might, though," Lily says, drawing out the last word. "You said they didn't figure it out with Trey until now. He's seventeen. What if Cooper *does* have dyslexia but no one ever figured it out?"

"And I'm the one who did? Come on, Lily."

"If he's managed to get along for years convincing everyone he doesn't care, or he's lazy, or whatever, there'd be no reason for anyone to look any deeper. And I know Cooper's got a soft spot about being dumb. What if he's just been rolling along, thinking he's not that smart?" Lily seems to think this is a possibility.

"But he *is* smart. That's why I thought... That's why I *assumed* there was something else. And I went into it angry because he wasn't sharing it with me. This is a mess." I put my head in my hands.

"Can't you explain that? Apologize?" My mother makes it sound so simple.

"He's not answering my calls, and he's ignoring my texts. And I basically told him I think something's wrong with him, Mama. What if he can't forgive that?" I can feel the tears coming on.

"You didn't say there's something wrong with him, Hadley, you said you understood why he is the way he is." My grandmother's words are true, but probably not enough to make a difference to Cooper.

"Well, you have to try. Give him a bit to cool off. He has

to come to the presentation. He can't ignore you forever."
Lily seems sure.

But I'm not. Cooper doesn't have to do anything he
doesn't want to do, and seeing me is probably at the top of
that list.

37

Cooper

"Didn't expect you to be here today. Don't trust me with your prize moonshine?" Eddie's got on one of his good-natured smiles, but I don't return it. His mouth turns down into a frown. "What bug got up your butt?"

"Tryin' to work, Eddie. That's all." Pinpricks of shame fan out over my neck. Being short with Eddie isn't going to fix my problem. And it obviously doesn't make me feel any better.

"So *sorry* to bother you." He starts to walk away but turns back toward me. "Hadley comin' in today? I need to ask her opinion about a few things." Of course Eddie picks today to start needing Hadley's help.

"I doubt it. Doubt we'll be seeing much of her from here on out." I keep my hands busy with the bottler, try to use that as an excuse to keep my eyes from meeting Eddie's.

"Aw, Cooper, what did you do?" He sounds exasperated, and I don't blame him. Usually it is me screwing things up. It's my specialty. That and then charming my way out of the situations I create. But this time I haven't done anything wrong except forget to protect myself. I won't let that happen again.

"I didn't do anything."

"Nothing? Think hard. Women are tough to figure out sometimes. Tell me what she said, and maybe we can figure it out together." I cannot imagine Eddie would ever be any help in rescuing a relationship, but I go ahead and give him the short version anyway.

"She asked me if I had a learning disability." I reach for another one of the fancy glass bottles Hadley picked out and fit the neck to the machine.

Eddie doesn't say anything for a second or two, and I begin to wonder if he's heard me. I'm about to repeat it when he finally clears his throat. "Did she mean it like an insult or something?"

"I don't think so. She was mad because I never told her." The clear liquid fills the bottle. Since this is a tiny batch, I'm doing the work by hand. Luckily it's the kind of job that's repetitive enough to be easy even with a heavy heart.

"Why didn't you tell her?" There's not a hint of sarcasm or joking in Eddie's question.

"Because I don't have a learning disability." I turn my angry face toward him. "Jesus, Eddie."

"You don't have to get all ornery. I just thought..." Eddie pulls his ball cap off his head and runs his fingers through his gray hair. "It isn't outside the realm of possibility."

"The *realm of possibility*? What are we now, hobbits? I don't have dyslexia or whatever. I'm a little dumb, that's all." I yank the full bottle from the nozzle harder than I should. Lord knows why it doesn't spill because it absolutely should, especially given the day I'm having.

"Never said you were dumb, Cooper. Lots of people have learning issues. That don't mean they're dumb. My grandson, Everett, he gets help at school for something like that. That boy ain't stupid and neither are you. Hadley didn't say you were stupid, did she?" Eddie crushes his hat in his hands as he waits for my answer.

"She didn't have to. I've always known I wasn't smart enough for her, but I was hoping I could keep it from her a bit longer, you know? That's selfish, though; she deserves somebody worthy of her." I brace myself for the pity I'll see on Eddie's face when I look up, but there's nothing like that at all reflected back at me. His wrinkled brow is set in a hard line, his mouth an angry pucker.

"Don't bother capping that one." Eddie grabs two glasses from the nearest shelf. "Come on out here with me and bring that bottle with you." He strides through the swinging saloon doors out to the front of the store. When he gets to the front door he turns the bolt and flips the open sign to tell the world we're closed.

I walk out carrying the open bottle. None of them have labels on them yet, since Hadley and I've been arguing over the name. She'd wanted something sophisticated, and I'd wanted something silly. There's our relationship encapsulated in one sentence. I'd laugh, but there's nothing humorous about it.

"Sit," Eddie orders, and I put my butt in the stool. Now is not the time to argue with Eddie even though I've got more moonshine to bottle and a hundred missing assignments I need to catch up on. He puts the empty glasses in front of me and takes the stool next to mine at the bar. "Pour."

"It's not even ten o'clock."

Eddie shoots me a look I've only ever seen him give to people who eat all the free samples at the farmers market.

"Fine." I pour us each enough for a taste and put the bottle on the bar top between us.

"We're gonna need more than that, Cooper. Go again." Eddie motions with his fingers toward the bottle.

"I don't see the need to—" Eddie silences me with his hand. I groan, but go ahead and put more liquor in our glasses. "It'll be your fault if I end up having to call one of my brothers for a ride home."

"I'll accept that responsibility." Eddie picks up his glass and holds it to the light. "That's damn near perfect, Cooper."

I look at the liquid in my glass. It's moonshine, not whiskey, so it doesn't have the color it would get from the barrel. It's got none of the flavors from the aging process either, so there's no char or caramel here other than what would have been in the ingredients. The Allen recipe isn't pure corn like some other moonshine. It's got a little malted barley in the mash. It could still use some tweaking to make it my own, but this first batch I made as close to the original as possible. I'm hoping my brothers will appreciate that.

Eddie takes a sip and closes his eyes. "I know this is only the first go, but you could enter this into any contest and do respectably." He takes another sip. "Smooth. Just a little burn."

"I know what you're trying to do." I fold my arms over my chest.

"I'm tryin' to enjoy some excellent moonshine." Eddie puts his glass back down on the bar. "You should have a little."

I begrudgingly bring my glass to my lips. I've already taste tested the hell out of it, so I know it's good. I also know I can make it better. It's still a little too sweet for my preference, but that can be fixed. And who's to say sweet isn't the way everyone else will like it? I'm willing to give people what they want.

"Not everyone can make shine like that, Cooper. Most

people can't make anything at all, much less something as good as that." Eddie takes another sip.

"Great. So I can make moonshine. That's not exactly the kind of thing you put on a resume, Eddie." I fight the urge to roll my eyes.

"It is if you're looking for a job at a distillery. If you want to prove you can *run* a distillery. Does it help you get a job manning the front desk at a hotel? Probably not. Do they care down at the Jiffy Lube? I doubt it." Eddie looks me full in the face. "But those aren't the jobs you want. Those are the jobs you've been taking, and I understand why, but they're not the ones for you."

I go to interrupt because I already know how this pep talk's going to go, but Eddie's not having any of that. He raises his weathered hand again and motions to my glass. "You don't do the other stuff well, but you do this *exceptionally* well. And there are plenty of other examples of things you can easily do that other people struggle with. School's not easy for you, but that's because of the way they set it up. It doesn't play to your strengths. Your grandpa always used to brag on you...tell everybody how you could build just about anything, figure out problems no one else could when it came to farm equipment. That's not the mark of an idiot, Cooper. Now maybe Hadley's right and there's a reason you aren't great at the stuff you need to do to get good grades, but look at you. You're finishing anyway. It took you a while, but you didn't give up. Didn't quit, even though it was hard."

"I don't know if taking fourteen years to finally finish my undergraduate degree is exactly something to celebrate, Eddie." I take another sip of my moonshine to keep from saying anything else. I'm still not feeling pride the way everyone thinks I should. Right now I'm full to the brim with shame, and the situation with Hadley's only intensified that.

"The hell it isn't," Eddie snaps. "Plenty of people give up on those things, and I know it's only a piece of paper, but it opens doors. And you and Hadley kept pushing until you made those doors open for you. So now you're giving up? I find that hard to believe. Never thought of you as a quitter."

"I don't think fighting for Hadley's going to make a difference. She's not supposed to be here with little dreams; she was supposed to be doing these big things. And now she knows for sure that I'm not the one to give her any of that. Hell, she thinks I can't read." I sigh and finish my drink.

"She doesn't think that," Eddie says, waving his hand like he can wave that thought away. "And she's been sittin' here in Mint Springs this whole time. Why do you think no one else has been able to help her make those big dreams come true?"

I shrug. How am I to know why Hadley's been waiting here?

"I think you and Miss Crawford got a little bit of meant to be. Now you get on out of here and figure out how to make that work. She hurt your pride, but she came at it from a good place. And if I remember correctly, you hurt her pride once upon a time too. I'll finish up your bottles. Now git." He makes like he's going to chase me, and I jump off my stool.

"I'm going, but I'm trusting you with my moonshine. No messing around."

"Tell that to yourself," Eddie calls over his shoulder as he goes through the swinging doors.

38

Hadley

"What are you still doing here?"

"I could ask you the same question." I push one of the old kitchen chairs away from the table. "Feel like sitting for a bit?"

Mindy settles herself in the chair across from me. "I can't stay long. I need to get back to Mama's to grab Caleb, and Devin'll be waiting on his dinner. I only came in because I thought I left my phone in here."

"You are a terrible liar."

"What part of that's a lie?" Mindy huffs. "I *do* need to get Caleb. And I should make dinner, although I don't think I have anything at home, so I'll need to stop by the store."

"And your phone?" I wait for my sister to admit her little white lie.

"It turns out it was in my bag the whole time." Mindy acts shocked. "But I noticed your car out front and saw the light was on. Shouldn't you go home, Hadley?"

"I'm just waiting a bit." I'm trying to get my courage up to go back to my apartment, knowing there's no possibility of

Cooper showing up with amnesia. That's the only way he'd be able to forgive me for the crazy way I acted this morning.

"Look, I know you're upset about Cooper, but, trust me, you're better off having him disappoint you now. If you two tried to make things work, you'd get hurt later on down the line when you had more invested. Better to cut your losses." Mindy gives me a self-satisfied look, and I see red.

"Cooper hasn't disappointed me, Mindy. Right now the only person I'm disappointed in is myself."

"How can you not be disappointed, Hadley? You've always been so smart, and here you go choosing a dummy. Think this through. You were right that he wasn't smart, and you need smart." Again Mindy gives me a knowing look.

"I never said Cooper wasn't smart." I am thoroughly regretting having Mindy anywhere within earshot when I was discussing my Cooper issues this morning. "He's one of the smartest men I know."

"You yourself said he's got some disability. Sorry for pointing out the obvious."

"Even if he does have dyslexia, I never should have brought it up like that. And, for your information, a learning disability doesn't mean dumb. It usually means very intelligent. And I'd appreciate you watching your word choice." I've done enough research to know what I'm talking about, and I've spent enough time with Cooper to be confident in my assessment of him.

"Well, I don't know if I should trust the opinion of someone who threw away her chance at Harvard. Maybe you're not the best judge of things."

"And you are? How's your fairy tale working out, Mindy?" It's a low blow, and one I regret the second I see my sister's face fall, even though throwing Harvard in my face was catty as hell.

"That is the ugliest thing you have *ever* said to me," Mindy whispers. "I am trying to help you. A relationship takes two people, Hadley, and I don't think Cooper's the right choice for you. Yes, my own marriage might not be perfect, but that doesn't mean I don't want something better for you. Cooper isn't good enough."

I think for a minute. "The thing is, Mindy, he is. He's more than good enough. He's not perfect, but who is? Certainly not me."

"He's hurt you before, Hadley, and he never explained that. I can't believe you took him back so easily. And now you're hurting again, and whose fault is that?"

I know Mindy thinks she's making her case, but she's only making me realize how much I want Cooper in my life. "It's *my* fault, Mindy. This time it's all my fault." I reach for my bag and push away from the table. "I need to get going, and you probably need to get to the store if Devin's going to get any dinner tonight."

"Devin won't be waiting on his dinner. He moved out."

"He what? When?" I sit back down. "Oh, Mindy." I cover my mouth with my hand. "And I just said...I'm so sorry."

"Don't be. You were right. There's no such thing as a fairy tale. And Cooper might not be Devin, but he's got his own baggage. You need to be sure you're ready for that." She massages her temples.

"Everybody's got baggage. You sure you want to go home? We could go over to Mama's and order a pizza. I can try to be less bitchy."

That at least gets a laugh out of Mindy.

"You, less bitchy? That'll be the day." Mindy stands. "I'm going to have to figure out how to do this on my own eventually. Might as well get started." She's almost to the front door when she turns back to look at me. "I've got nothing against

Cooper. I just want you to be sure you're making choices for the right reasons."

"I know. And I appreciate it." I do appreciate it, even if I'm going to ignore every piece of Mindy's advice. Every bone in my body is telling me I need to fix things with Cooper, and that's what I get started on the second Mindy's taillights disappear.

I call him once before I lock up the salon. No answer. My message sounds shaky but hopeful.

I call again when I get to my apartment. This time I try more contrite.

The third call comes after three glasses of wine and focuses on how we still have to work together on this presentation even if he never wants to see me again. Even this dramatic message doesn't get a response. No returned call, no text, not even a smoke signal. He most certainly doesn't appear at my door to sweep me off my feet. I fall into bed with a sinking feeling I might not get the chance to make things right with Cooper, reasons be damned.

39

Cooper

"What are you doing out here in the dark?" My brother's voice cuts through what had been a somewhat enjoyable silence.

"Thinking." It's not a lie, exactly, although my brain's been chugging along without any discernible thought for a while now.

"Thinking about how you should call Hadley?" Charlie plops down next to me on the porch steps.

"Actually, no. I was thinking I need to get a junkyard dog to keep trespassers off my property."

"Come on now. You don't want a dog chasing friends and family away, do you? What would be the fun in that? And it would mean no one could deliver your dinner." He hands me a plate covered with cling film, the bottom still warm. "We missed you at supper. Mae's worried you're going to starve."

"That's the last thing she should be worried about." I reach for the glass of whiskey I've been sipping on. "You sticking around for a bit? I think I have one other clean glass."

"You have hooch out here?" Charlie's eyes light up. "Hell yeah, I'll take some."

"Don't get too excited, we're not trying to get drunk, dumbass. This is good stuff. For sipping. Not for shots like you're at Bootlegger." I stand, aware of the strain on my back from sitting on the hard, wooden steps. I walk through the house until I get to the kitchen. It's getting closer to being finished and is starting to look like I'll eventually be able to move in. Cabinets and countertops will be coming in soon. I take my extra glass from the plastic bin I'm using for supplies and grab the bottle of whiskey.

Charlie's spread out on the steps, his long legs stretched out in front of him. "When are you getting chairs for out here? I thought that and the hot tub were the first things you were going to take care of."

"Roof trumps hot tub." I think about Hadley's porch swing and get a pang of longing I have to will away before Charlie can see anything's wrong. I hand him a glass of whiskey. "Taste this. I managed to find a bottle of Elijah Craig Barrel Proof."

"I don't even know what that means." Charlie raises the glass to his lips, takes a sip, and then gives his lips a smack. "That's pretty good. You're really getting into this whiskey stuff."

"You could say that." I'm afraid to let Charlie in on too much before the presentation.

The presentation. *Shit.*

"Lily said you and Hadley had a falling out." Charlie isn't wasting any time.

"You could say that." I sip more of the whiskey, happy to let the cinnamon and vanilla dominate my thoughts instead of my problems with Hadley. I'm concentrating on the hint of apple when Charlie speaks again.

"What would *you* say?"

"I'd say Hadley finally found my soft spot." I let the slight burn of the whiskey keep me from saying anything more.

"And that's bad?" Charlie's serious. "I'm no expert here, but you didn't think she'd go on forever thinking you didn't have any flaws, did you? If she loves you, then she'd want to see the soft spots. Everybody's got them, Cooper, might as well share with people who care about you."

Love. Hadley doesn't love me. Shouldn't love me, not if she knows what's good for her. "I think this is going to be a deal breaker."

Charlie lets out a *humph*. "For you? Because Lily seemed to think whatever it was wasn't doing that for Hadley."

"Lily tell you the details?" I don't think I can bear having my family talking about what happened like it's some salacious gossip. More of that familiar shame washes over me.

"No. She said Hadley said something and was regretting it. And I didn't come here to ask you for specifics; I'm just checking to make sure you're okay. But we can drink. I'm fine with that too." He raises his glass toward me.

"Let me ask you something." I hesitate; of all of us, Charlie's the most easygoing. He's second only to me in the good-times guy category. He's probably not the best brother to spill my guts to, but he's the only one here right now, and the whiskey's loosening my tongue enough to take a chance.

"Shoot." I can still see Charlie's smile in the dark. He's always smiling, hardly ever serious or angry. Only really sad when the situation's dire, definitely not my target audience for this conversation.

"Would you say I'm smart?" I brace myself for peals of laughter or a punch in the arm.

"Smart? Sure. Not book smart, maybe, but plenty smart just the same."

"Not book smart? What's that mean?"

Charlie doesn't even take time to think. "School stuff, you know. But you never really cared about any of that anyway. Do you have more of this? I'm getting low over here." He waves his almost empty glass at me.

"You thought I didn't care about school?" I reach for his glass to refill it, even though I should give him the lecture about enjoying it first. The liquor glugs into the tumbler, and Charlie ends up with a generous pour.

"Nah, you seemed more interested in other stuff, like school didn't interest you. Like it was taking up time you could've been spending doing something else."

"But you didn't think it was because I was stupid?" I wait for the inevitable confirmation that my brother has always known I was as dumb as a box of rocks.

Charlie shakes his head. "I'd never say you were stupid, Cooper. Not in a million years. Why are you asking these questions?"

I let out a breath. "Because that's what Hadley thinks."

"Hadley said she thought you were stupid? Why the hell would she say that?" The anger in Charlie's voice spills out onto the porch steps.

"She didn't say it like that exactly," I clarify. "She thought maybe I had dyslexia."

"Do you?" Charlie's genuinely asking.

"No." I pause. "I don't think so."

"You don't sound very sure."

"The thing is, I did a little research, and maybe I do. But I'd know that, right? They'd have figured that out when I was in elementary school or something." Then I wouldn't be here wondering if Hadley was right when it comes to my issues.

"You'd think they would have, but you never know. You know who should know, though?" Charlie finishes the liquid in his glass and offers it to me again.

"Who?" I put more of my coveted whiskey into his glass, aiming to give him less than before.

"Mom. You should call her."

"Call her?" I rarely talk to my mother. And never about difficult things. Once our parents divorced, that relationship sort of fell apart. She and my father spent so much time ripping each other to shreds there wasn't much left of either of them once they were finally free of each other.

"She'll know about you and elementary school. If anyone ever said anything about any of that, she'd be the one to remember." Charlie leans back on his elbows and tilts his head to the night sky. "I think maybe you did pick the best spot."

"Of course I did." I let out a huff.

"Not too stupid to figure *that* out."

I give Charlie a shove and don't even mind spilling his whiskey.

40

Hadley

The flowers are at Eddie's when I make my way through the front door—a million peonies and tulips and hydrangeas, along with all the greenery I'll need to make them look fabulous. I glance around the warehouse and hope Cooper's hiding out in the back.

"Cooper? Eddie?" My voice echoes off the walls. No answer. I'm pulling out my phone when Eddie comes through the swinging doors, his hands full of plastic tubing.

"Hey there, Hadley. Wasn't expecting you here so early." He puts all the tubes down on the bar. "Don't worry, I'm not gonna leave that there." His smile fades when he sees I'm not wearing one.

"I thought I'd get a head start, maybe have a chance to talk to Cooper before we did all the final touches." I look over Eddie's shoulder. "Is he back there?"

"No, darlin'. He's not." Eddie looks almost as disappointed as I feel. "I'm guessing he was here earlier since he moved all that inside, but he's not here now."

My shoulders sag. I had thought Cooper would have to

show up for this. He's been avoiding me for the past two days but here he'd have to talk to me. There'd be no way to ignore my questions—or my apologies. "Did he tell you if he was planning on coming by later?"

"I haven't seen him. He snuck in and out this morning without a word. Didn't even check on the moonshine."

"That's not like him." Now I'm more worried than ever. What if Cooper doesn't show up to help finish the work here? What if he doesn't show up for the presentation?

"It isn't, but he's got a lot on his mind." Eddie doesn't meet my eyes.

"He told you."

Eddie fidgets a bit. "He did. Not all of it, but enough. He needs a little time, Hadley."

"You must think I'm terrible," I sniffle, tears already starting to fall.

"No, no," Eddie assures me, patting my arm. "I know how sensitive Cooper can be about his intelligence, or what he sees as a lack of it. And to have you be the one to question it? Well, that hit him hard, that's for sure."

"But I wasn't questioning his intelligence. I really thought he was keeping the fact that he had a learning challenge from me. It didn't occur to me he might not have one or might never have considered it." I have put my foot in my mouth big time with this. How can Cooper forgive me for being selfish enough to make something so clearly about him all about me? In trying to keep my heart safe, I've gone and broken Cooper's. Although maybe his heart's not broken, maybe it's just wounded pride that's got him upset. That might be worse for me in the long run—it'd be pretty easy to walk away from me if his heart isn't involved.

"I know you didn't mean to hurt his feelings, but he's hurt all the same. Give him a minute to sort through all of that. He'll come around." Eddie's little head nod doesn't give me much hope.

"You think so?" I want Eddie to have the answers, to be able to tell me Cooper will eventually forgive me.

"I'm pretty sure." That doesn't sound definitive. "What do you need help with today? I'm all yours for a few hours. Put me to work." He rubs his hands together like he can't wait to start.

"I think I can handle most of it. I'll let you know if I need an extra set of hands." I dismiss Eddie, because the only person I really want to help is Cooper. I can do the work myself, and I don't waste time moping. I get right to work moving the flowers from the buckets of water to the Mason jars I've brought with me.

"Wow! This looks amazing."

"You aren't supposed to see it until tomorrow," I wail. The surprise appearance of Lily coming through the front door shouldn't make me feel so sad.

"I thought you might need a little moral support. I'll pretend I've never seen it when we all walk in tomorrow. Promise."

"Cooper's not coming, is he?" If Lily's here, she must know something I don't.

"Not today. He's trying to work through some things. He'll come around, though." She gives my arm an encouraging squeeze.

"That's what Eddie said. You two operating from the same playbook?" It isn't comforting to have everyone saying the same thing, especially when I know it might be wishful thinking. And when I'm not seeing any evidence of it from Cooper. "I can't believe how badly I've screwed this up."

"It isn't over yet, Hadley," Lily assures me.

"But why couldn't I just have kept my big mouth shut?"

Or at least tried to use some of that tact I'm always complaining no one else has?

"That wouldn't have been you, and Cooper knows it. Everybody expects you to speak your mind and that's what you did. You were off-base, sure, but you weren't holding back." Lily laughs. "Now let's get to work."

Not holding back? It may have seemed like I wasn't, but in reality, I was doing my best not to get burned again, trying to make sure Cooper couldn't make me feel small. Instead of waiting for him to surprise me, I'd made damn sure he couldn't. Letting out my own insecurities and fears looked like my usual stubbornness to everyone else.

And probably to Cooper, too.

"What else are we doing back here? I like the flowers, that's a nice touch." Lily might as well be talking to herself, because I barely hear her. Instead, I'm thinking about how a simple apology isn't going to make up for anything where Cooper's concerned.

"I need your help with something."

"That *is* what I'm here for." Lily looks at me and wrinkles her forehead. "Duh, Hadley."

"No, I need your help with something for Cooper." I hope I look contrite enough to convince Lily to get on board.

"That I would be more than happy to help you with." Lily links her arm with mine. "Tell me all about this big idea."

I'm not so sure it's big, but hopefully it's genuine enough to make Cooper forgive me.

41

Cooper

"What are you doing out here? Shouldn't you be at Eddie's?" Mae's hands on her hips have me snapping to attention.

"I've got some chores to do around here. Don't want these stairs to give you and Sadie any trouble." I go back to hammering down the loose board I've been neglecting for too long.

"That can wait, Cooper," Mae yells over the persistent hammering I had thought would put an end to this discussion. "While Sadie and I appreciate you making sure our front steps are as safe as can be, I think maybe today Hadley needs a little of your help." Mae isn't going to be easily convinced to let me use the farm as an excuse today.

"Where'd you hear that?" I keep the hammer poised to finish what I started.

"Eddie McDonald has been known to give me updates on you from time to time." Mae stares down at me like the lead detective in one of those cable TV cop shows. "I know a little about how things have been going down there."

"I'm going to need to have a little talk with Eddie about his gossipy ways." I play it off like teasing, but you can bet I'm going to have a word with Eddie. Tattling on me to Mae? He's going to get an earful about that. "I didn't think you knew Eddie."

"I've known Eddie since before you were born. You think in this small town I don't know just about everybody? And I probably spent more time with Eddie than Jefferson ever did. Your grandpa might have been the one to introduce the two of you, but who do you think introduced him to Eddie in the first place?" The accompanying *harrumph* has me afraid to ask any more questions, even though my head's full of them. *Mae and Eddie? Friends?*

"And don't go inventing your own stories over there. I think this thing with you and Hadley's reminded all of us of the importance of getting the facts before we start talking." Mae settles herself on the step next to me. "Put that hammer away and sit for a minute." She pats the spot next to her.

Spilling my guts to my great aunt is not at all what I had planned for today, but I don't think she's going to give me much of a choice. I give up on my repairs and sit next to her. I wait for her to give me a lecture, but the quiet grows between us. It's not an uneasy silence, but eventually the waiting gets the best of me.

"So—"

"There is something about the farm in the morning, isn't there?" Mae takes a deep breath. "Another day to be thankful to be alive."

"I guess."

"I try to appreciate the time we've been given. Not waste it." Mae gives me a nod. "Time goes by fast. Faster than you think."

"Yes, ma'am." I can't argue with that even though Mae seems to think I might.

"Heard you might have talked to your mama." Mae says it as much to the chickens in the yard as she does to me. They scratch around in the dirt in front of us.

"I did." It was the kind of conversation I would have put off forever if I could have, but after talking to Charlie, I knew I wouldn't be able to get out of it. I'd have to call eventually and poke around at that old wound.

"Was she able to answer your questions?" I get the feeling Mae already knows all about what my mother told me, probably has known for years.

"She was, not that I was happy to hear what she had to say." As soon as she'd picked up the phone my mother had been contrite. It isn't often that I call her, and I'll admit that probably makes me a less-than-stellar son. She is my mother, after all, and she can't change the way things happened with my father any more than I can.

"You want to share any of that?" Mae's gentle prodding is the same as it's always been. She's always been a safe space. Still, the things my mother told me are painful to talk about. "Might help ease the burden a bit."

"Hadley was right." I squeeze the handle of the hammer hard enough to imagine it cracking in my hand.

Mae cocks her head, looking like Marlon Brando the rooster when he hears the sound of the feed in the can in the morning. "How so?" she asks, and I know she already knows.

"The school wanted to test me in third grade. Thought my reading difficulties might have been something more. But Dad didn't want me in *special classes* so nothing ever came of it." My mother had apologized and apologized. She had tried her best, had worked to give me extra help at home, but my father had been adamant. No testing. No special help that might make me look like I was different.

"How's that making you feel?" Mae's hand comes out to pat mine. It's a reassuring gesture that keeps me talking.

"Confused. Why would he do that? I've thought for years I wasn't as smart as other people. I was already struggling in school. There was no reason to make it more difficult." The anger that keeps rising up in me threatens to surface again. "I made so many decisions based on limitations I gave myself. But I researched, and dyslexia doesn't mean dumb. Not at all."

"I think he was doing what he thought was best. Your father isn't always the most thoughtful man, but when it comes to you boys, I do think he tried to make decisions with your best interests at heart."

"But if he wanted to keep me from feeling different, that's not what happened. I'm a grown man, and I just found out something that changes everything." I turn the hammer over in my hand. "No matter how hard I tried, it never made a difference, and I knew that was something to be ashamed of—something to hide. I even pushed Hadley away the first time because she'd eventually see it. She'd figure it out and realize I wasn't enough."

Mae regards me with a sadness I haven't seen in her in a while. "When you came back to Mint Springs? That's a shame. A real shame. You can't be afraid to be genuine with people, especially the ones you love. Did you explain that to Hadley?"

"No, ma'am. She thinks I walked away, forgot about her. I couldn't tell her the real reason. I thought she'd be better off without me standing in her way."

"Standing in her way? Cooper Allen, you cannot think

that." Mae shakes her head. "You have plenty to offer, and I think Hadley agrees. What's she say about all of this?"

"I haven't told her. She figured it out all on her own, she doesn't need me to confirm it."

"While she might not need you to confirm it, I think she might need to know you forgive her for the way she brought it up." Mae doesn't need to tell me she's been talking to more than just Eddie. "Only a suggestion. Now I need to get back to the garden. Those weeds won't pull themselves, you know." Mae stands and brushes the dust off her backside. "Don't ruin something you want because your pride got hurt. Hadley's separate from the way you feel about the rest. Think about that."

And that's what I do as I walk down the gravel road from Sadie and Mae's house toward the old barn. As the weathered gray structure comes into view, my mind can't help but flash back to all the summers I spent here on the farm. Back then there were cows and horses and plenty of hay in this barn. There were also four original walls. That was one of the main reasons I initially decided to help Chance as much as I did, discovering that someone had snuck onto the property and stolen an entire wall from our barn. Now, there's a new front on the thing, put there with my own two hands. I had a little help from my brother, of course, but putting the barn back together definitely made it clear to me I wasn't ready to give this farm up.

But there's another reason.

I pull one of the doors open and walk inside. Even though Chance and Lily have been using this building as an office for a while now, there's still the unmistakable sweet smell of hay once I close the door behind me. When I think about my family's history there's plenty of it right here. It's the first building that was constructed on the farm and it's the only one made from wood milled from the property. As kids my brothers and I worked in this barn, played hide and seek in the stalls, and basically ran wild every chance we got. Once we were older, the barn was more of a secret place, one where I brought Hadley.

I climb up into the hayloft, nervous the ladder might not actually hold me. There's no hay in here now, of course, because there aren't any animals to feed. And even when there was, this wasn't the most comfortable place. That didn't stop us though, because privacy was at a premium on this farm. I'd been terrified to make my move, nervous Hadley'd shoot me down. I might have talked a good game, but I was as green as they come when feelings were involved. And with Hadley I had feelings—big feelings that filled my chest and made me light-headed. The kind of feelings that made me want more than I knew it was realistic to hope for. I walk to the back of the barn and run my hands along the wood there. It doesn't take too many passes to find what I'm looking for. My fingers eventually find the grooves there in the old boards right where I carved them.

My initials and Hadley's separated by a heart.

CA and HC carved forever into the one place that meant forever to me. Luckily this wasn't the wall the thieves carted off. I'd been surprised at my relief when I'd seen the place for myself. An entire wall of a barn doesn't go missing every day, and we'd never found out for sure who'd taken it, but this memory was still where it was supposed to be. Hadley'd laughed when I'd done it all those years ago, concentrating on getting the lines as close to perfect as I could with my pocket knife. She'd still been all mussed up from rolling round up here, her lips swollen from my kisses and her cheeks pink with that flush of new love.

Then I'd walked away and tried to forget, but that wasn't

going to happen. I'd tried to pretend I had, but even that had proven impossible. Rain starts to fall on the tin roof, and now I've got more than one decision to make. The sound soothes me, and I'm more than happy to settle myself down on the edge of the loft and let my legs dangle. Hadley hurt me, that's for sure, but she thought I'd been lying, and I've given her reasons not to trust me.

You can't be afraid to be genuine with people, especially the ones you love.

Mae's words rattle around in my brain like a loose marble. I haven't given myself a chance to be genuine with *most* of those people. My who-gives-a-shit persona hasn't done much to really protect me, it's only served to keep me from connecting with anyone. It's kept me from really letting people in, and Hadley's been getting the worst of that. If I don't change all that right now, nothing else is going to change either.

So I'm going to start doing things differently.

I take a deep breath. "What do you think about that?" My life-changing decision makes no difference to these four walls. But it'll make all the difference to me. And maybe to Hadley if I do it right.

42

Hadley

I'm rearranging the flowers for the millionth time when Cooper walks through the front door. I'm not sure if the feeling that washes over me is relief or fear, but my stomach drops and then rights itself with plenty of time for me to try to put a neutral smile on my face either way. Cooper's wearing exactly what we discussed when we were putting the final touches on today. I can't help but admire the way he fills out the suit he's wearing. We'd both agreed we wanted to look as professional as possible, especially since this is his pitch for the distillery. His family might not know it yet, but they're about to hear the world's best business idea, and I'm hoping they're blown away, not only by our preparation but by Cooper's passion for the project.

"I wasn't sure you'd come." I don't let the apprehension I'm feeling keep me from saying it. My big mouth may have gotten me in trouble, but I'm not going to pretend everything's fine.

Cooper's face clouds. "I'm sorry you thought I'd let you down, Hadley. I would never do that on purpose. In fact, I'm going to try my best to never do that again." He sounds sincere and more contrite than he should when I know I should be bearing some of the responsibility here.

"I know you wouldn't, I wasn't meaning to imply—"

Cooper cuts me off. "The thing is, I have before. I know that. And I need to explain why so you understand why I did the things I did." He gestures to one of the seats at the barrel tables I've set up.

"Cooper, I really need to—"

"Hadley, you are trying my patience." Cooper smiles as he says it though, and I start to think things might not be as bad as I thought. "You have got to let me get this out." He reaches for my hand. "I'm going to give you a chance to talk, I promise."

"Okay." I roll my lips between my teeth and try to keep them there.

Cooper gives my hand a squeeze. "You were right. Or close to it, at least. I might very well have dyslexia. It was suspected, but I've never been tested. I'm working on getting that taken care of, because it would answer a lot of questions I've had for a while. So, while I was upset when you first brought it up, it's helped me to get a new perspective on some issues I've had since I was a kid."

Even trying to clamp my mouth shut, I can't help but cut in. "I should never have said it that way, though. I made it all about me, Cooper, and I didn't even think about how it might make you feel. Or if I might be wrong." My bottom lip trembles a bit. Cooper might have thought I was a selfish person before, but now he's got confirmation.

"Oh, I was pissed at first, I'm not gonna lie, but that's because you hit on something I've tried to hide from you, Hadley. So even if your delivery was off, you'd figured out the problem." Cooper tilts his head back a bit and looks at the ceiling. "This is hard for me to admit, but I've been keeping something from you for years."

"That doesn't sound good." I'm a ball of nervous energy now, unsure of what Cooper's about to confess.

"I've spent most of my life thinking I was dumb. Definitely not as smart as other people. When you and I got together, and I realized how smart you are, I got scared. That's why I disappeared—why I pretended not to remember you—because I thought once you figured it out you wouldn't want anything to do with me. If anyone figured it out, they'd think less of me, but having you know my limitations... I couldn't stand that. I built up these walls to protect myself, and that meant not being honest with you." Cooper's hazel eyes meet mine. "But that stops right now."

I can barely breathe. This is the part I've been dreading, the part where Cooper tells me it's over. I exposed his worst fear, and now he can't forgive me. I blink away the beginning of what is sure to be a river of tears. But those tears are competing with another feeling rising in my chest. If Cooper can't handle being truthful with me, then it's for the best that we walk away now, before I've made a fool of myself and confessed my feelings. I have to be able to trust him, and I can't have him hiding when things get tough.

"Starting now, I'm going to be open with you. With everybody. And that starts by telling you the truth. I'm in love with you, Hadley, and I'm not keeping things from you anymore."

"What did you say?" I startle.

"That I'm not keeping things from you anymore?"

"No, before that." *Cooper Allen is in love with me?*

"I should have set that up better, I guess. I'm not great at this yet." Cooper slides a hand around to the back of his neck and squeezes. "I've been in love with you since our hayloft days, Hadley. Maybe even before that, and I'm ready to make sure everyone knows. So get ready, because I'm all set to make you fall in love with me too." He gives me that cocky grin, and I know everything's going to be fine.

"What makes you think you can make that happen?" I keep my hand in his and feel his grip tighten on my fingers.

"Well, you know I like a challenge, but I think you might be a little bit in love with me already." He raises an eyebrow, and as much as I'd love to keep him guessing, this isn't a time to hold back.

"I might be. Just a little bit," I confess. "And I'm a whole lot sorry about how I accused you of lying to me. I really have felt awful about that, Cooper. You thinking you aren't smart enough or that you needed to hide things from me..." The tears I've been holding in start to spill over. "You have to know you're more than a report card, more than what they told you you were."

"You know that's the same for you, right? I'm sorry if I made you feel less than when I came back here. I was scared and selfish, but I'm trying not to be now." Cooper stands and pulls me into his arms, wrapping me up tight. I relax into his embrace and go ahead and take a chance.

"Cooper?"

"Yeah?" he whispers into my hair.

"I might love you a lot."

The clapping's still ringing in my ears as Cooper and I go to get the bottles of moonshine we've made. Our presentation's been well-received, if the faces of our family and friends are any indication. Cooper's brothers have been giving each other looks through the whole thing. If this didn't get wheels turning in their heads, nothing will. Cooper's presentation style is more commanding than I'd expected, and he sounded every bit the expert as we went through our business proposal. Luckily we haven't had any technical issues—a miracle for one of these online classes if ever I've seen one—and we're right on time to finish up with a question and answer period before we sign off. Our classmates will have to go without the hooch to loosen their tongues, but we'll be giving generous samples to the live audience here.

I grab the tray of glasses and hope Cooper likes the surprise I planned for him. I needed a little help to pull it off, and before our talk this morning I was thinking it would be my only opportunity to show him how sorry I was and how much I'd been thinking about him. Now I'm thinking this will be the icing on the cake.

"We have a treat for those of you lucky enough to be here with us today. A little bit of a thank you for coming to our presentation and a way to show you we're serious." Cooper clasps his hands together. "With Eddie's help, Hadley and I made a batch of our own moonshine using the old Allen family recipe. We're going to give out some samples here in a minute, but before we start serving and answering any questions y'all might have, I'd like to take a minute to thank Eddie for letting us use his distillery and for teaching me everything I need to know about more than just distilling."

Eddie ducks his head but accepts the hoots and hollers of the small crowd. Chance puts his fingers in his mouth and whistles loudly. Lily's smiling beside him, ready for my big reveal.

"And I'd like to express my gratitude to Hadley. She's been a great sport through all of this, even though we both had our doubts about working together. There aren't words for what she means to me." The crowd *ahhhs*, and I catch my mother dabbing a bit at the corners of her eyes. She and my grandmother have gone all out today. You'd think they'd been invited to the Country Music Awards and not a virtual final for an online class. "That's why I named this first batch of our moonshine after her." Cooper holds up a bottle, the words *Hadley's Happiness* clearly visible on the label. "I thought about *Hadley's Hooch*, but I've been told if I want to be taken seriously, I need to act that way on occasion." He winks at me.

"Wait, no!" All faces turn toward me, probably surprised by my reaction. "*I* named the moonshine after Cooper." I look at Lily and then at Eddie, both of them laughing so hard they're crying. I reach under the table in front of us and produce my own bottle of moonshine. My label's more masculine than the one Cooper's created. I wanted it to look like a prohibition-era bottle to call back to the beginning of the Allen family recipe. *Cooper's Dream* stands out in the middle of my design. Eddie and Lily helped me to put the whole thing together and were sworn to secrecy. Apparently they did the same thing for Cooper.

"The two of you can never agree on anything," Eddie chokes out, and Lily agrees. Those traitors.

"I think we can agree on one thing." Cooper looks down at me and smiles. We've both come up with what we thought was the best way to show each other we cared—and we chose the same way. You can't argue with that.

"I think we can," I answer, and then kiss him like I mean it.

EPILOGUE

Cooper

"If there's ever been a better graduation party, I'd like to hear about it," Chance announces from his spot by the fire pit. It's warm enough for everyone to be outside without it, but the s'more station's getting a good deal of use. And it is nice to snuggle up by the fire, especially with one of the multiple specialty whiskeys my brothers have purchased for the celebration. *Hadley's Happiness/Cooper's Dream* is on the menu too. Eventually we'll come up with a better name, but for now we've got competing labels jockeying for position on the table we've set up as a bar out here in the barn.

Although calling this a barn doesn't do it justice. Chance and Lily did get married here, and we've shown we can dress the place up for a party. That's part of the reason we all agreed a restaurant and a space to hold events would work out here. Tonight the place is strung with fairy lights, and filled with the people Hadley and I love most, all here to celebrate the fact that we finally made it happen. The giant *Congratulations, Graduates* banner has been a long time coming, but doing this with Hadley is making it so much sweeter. I look over at her on the opposite side of the barn, deep in conversation with Lily. It's hard to believe she's all mine now.

"I doubt there's ever been a better party than this." I tip back the rest of my drink. "Who needs another?"

"Before we get too deep in the whiskey, we need to give you your gift." Chance motions for the rest of my brothers.

"Y'all didn't need to get me anything. This party's plenty, not to mention putting up with me every day."

"Maybe we didn't, but we've all agreed this is something you deserve." My brothers crowd around me, moving me over to the edge of the barn and the table where earlier we'd gorged ourselves on fried chicken. "Sit for a second."

I sit, but not without some reservations. Usually, having my brothers being this nice to me means trouble. They've thrown this party for me and Hadley, were more than helpful with finishing up my house, and had only compliments for my business plan. Now would be the time for them to shove a pie in my face or something.

"We all talked about this, and we think this is the perfect place for it." Chance unrolls a ream of paper out in front of me, smoothing the edges.

I look at the plans in front of me. We've been obsessing over the designs for the farm—arguing over where to put this and how big to make that. I've looked at these drawings a million times, so I let my eyes do a quick pass, unsure of why my brothers would think right now's a great time to hash out these details again.

And then I see it.

Right where we're sitting now, there's something new. Instead of the old barn, there's a new building. One labeled *Cooper's Distillery*. My head snaps up from the plans to look at my brothers. All three of them are wearing the kind of grins I usually hate to see, only tonight I couldn't be happier to be looking at these ugly faces.

"Is this a joke?" I tap my finger on the spot where my imaginary distillery sits.

"Why would we joke about that?" Cade asks. "Your idea's a good one, Cooper."

"And it fits in perfectly with the other things we've been planning," Charlie offers. "Don't know why you held out on us for so long."

"But it's expensive. Too expensive." I imagine having the spot I'm sitting on now actually become the distillery Hadley and I planned. It'd be no small undertaking.

"We looked at the business plan you and Hadley made, and it's actually not that bad. Being able to use this space for tastings and tours and smaller events makes sense." Chance puts a hand on my shoulder. "Financially we can make it work, and it'll be a nice addition for the restaurant."

"Not to mention the fact that it tells a story. It's a great way to pull the place together and start branding. You and Hadley nailed it when it comes to all that." Cade shrugs. He knows more about that side of things than any of us.

I take a deep breath. It's really happening.

"We figured the barn's the perfect spot. We'll need you to decide how to go from there—you're the expert on what needs to be done to make the space work. We can use the existing structure or incorporate it into a new design..." Chance gives my shoulder a squeeze. "Congratulations."

I get a lump in my throat I know I won't be able to swallow, and I'm not sure I'd want to even if I could. I look at the faces of my younger brothers, all three looking back at me with nothing but love and support. I pull Chance into a bear hug first, slapping him on the back hard enough to have him coughing. Charlie and Cade get added to the scrum, and eventually it's one big mess of Allens wiping our eyes and laughing.

"Enough of that," I joke, and we all pretend we never let our emotions get the best of us. I straighten up and clear my throat. "I need to go tell my girl the good news, and one of y'all needs to keep an eye on Mae. She and Eddie are sitting awfully close over there." All eyes turn toward our great aunt and Eddie snuggled up by the fire pit. He's helping her roast a marshmallow, their heads bent together.

"What in the world?" Charlie looks at them with curiosity. "Cade, I'm feeling a hankering for graham crackers and chocolate. How 'bout you?"

Once they're off, I turn toward Chance. "Thanks for making all this happen."

"You're making it happen too, Cooper. I couldn't do any of it without all of you, and I wouldn't want to. It's family first, no matter what. Now go find Hadley." He gives me one more hug that has me wiping my eyes again. *Damn allergies.*

Hadley's not hard to find. I follow the sound of her laughter, and in a few steps I'm scooping her up and holding her tight.

"Excuse me, ladies." Her mother and grandmother are dressed to the nines, as usual—sparkling like a pair of disco balls out here in the twinkling lights of the barn. "I need to borrow Hadley for a few minutes." They shoo us away, and even Mindy manages to give me a smile. So far this night's perfect, and I'm about to try to make it even better.

"Where are we going?" Hadley lets me lead her away from the crowd.

"I need to show you something." I put her in my truck, plant a kiss on her lips, and start the drive down to my house. It isn't long before we see the porch light shining in the distance. The place is finished now, and I'm set to move in in the next few days.

"I cannot get over this house, Cooper. It turned out even prettier than I thought it would. You did such a great job." Having Hadley compliment me like that makes my chest damn near burst with happiness. And these days I try to take those compliments for what they are. No more trying to lessen the things I'm good at by focusing on those I struggle with.

I help Hadley down from the truck and bring her up onto the front porch. The night sky's clear, and you can see a million stars from here. I take Hadley's hands in mine. "I made you something."

"Interesting..." Hadley tilts her head. "And you had to bring me out here to show it to me?"

I shrug. "It lives here." I take her hand and bring her to the edge of the porch, wait to see if she'll notice the new addition.

When she finally does her hands fly to her mouth. "A swing?"

"Want to try it out?" I've got it all set up with pillows and a blanket, so it looks like something out of a magazine. I hold the chain so it doesn't move while she's getting settled.

"Are you testing this too?" Hadley pats the space next to her.

I sit and wait for her to notice the most important part.

"You really made this?" She runs her hands along wooden swing, pausing when her fingers make contact with the middle of the board closest to the top. She blinks, then pulls her fingertips over the spot again. "Is this...?"

"From the barn." I pulled the old board from the structure last week. Hadley had wanted a swing for this porch, and I'm hoping this is the first of many times we sit out here together.

"Our initials? I thought you'd forgotten." Hadley's voice is soft, vulnerable. We've still got a ways to go to heal all the old hurts. "Now every time I come to visit you I can sit out here and see them."

"I'm hoping you're going to be doing more than visiting."

Hadley's surprised face lifts toward mine. "What does that mean?"

"It means I'm hoping you'll move in here. I need somebody to enjoy this swing with me." I try not to sound too hopeful. If Hadley says no it'll crush me, but I don't want to move too fast if she's not ready. I'm not asking for forever yet, but I'd like to start moving in that direction.

"You want me to move into your house?"

"Our house. And I need someone to help me open a distillery, since I just found out we're opening one for real."

"You did? You are?" Her eyes are wide, always full of excitement when good things happen to me. Hadley's squeal fills the air. She dives into my arms.

"Is that a yes?"

"Of course that's a yes. I cannot wait to get started on this adventure with you." Hadley barely gets the words out before I crush my mouth to hers.

This moment here? Worth all the burn.

ACKNOWLEDGMENTS

Thank you all for reading *Make It Burn*. I hope you loved it. Hadley started out as the main focus of this book—because who doesn't love feisty Hadley—but I kind of fell in love with Cooper a little bit along the way. I started out knowing he was going to have a learning challenge, but I'd underestimated how hard it would be to write the inner workings of that. Here at my house we've got dyslexia and dysgraphia and plenty of bruised egos to show for it. Cooper's a fictional character, of course, but he's informed not only by my own children, but by countless other kids I've worked with. It's always the hardest when the issues is caught late. I've seen plenty of parents have that "aha moment" when their child is diagnosed and suddenly so many of their own struggles make sense. So thank you to all those warriors battling it out with their homework every night, and to all the parents trying to do what's best.

Thank you also to my editor Kiezha Ferrell for coming to the rescue. This is our first time working together and it could not have gone more smoothly. Your suggestions were spot on and made the book better. I appreciate you!

Thank you to Austin Ryan for her proofreading skills and ability to catch all sorts of mistakes I never even see. Without you there would be more typos going out into the world.

Thank you to Kate Farlow for another beautiful cover and for her continued flexibility. And for recommending Kiezha. That was a good call.

As always, thank you to my teenagers. There's no man chest on this cover, but I'm sure I've found plenty of other ways to embarrass all of you even without it. Thanks for listening to story ideas and enduring the endless things that go into romance writing. Love you all big.

ABOUT THE AUTHOR

Jessie Harper writes steamy, contemporary romance with a slightly Southern flavor. Originally from Nashville, Tennessee, she has lived all over the world—from Europe to Asia. She currently resides in Park City, Utah with her husband, three children, and more rescue animals than she ever intended. She appreciates a nice glass of whiskey, homegrown tomatoes, and well-delivered sarcasm. She hopes to never have to "bless your heart."

For updates and more visit www.jessieharper.com. Or sign up for Jessie's newsletter so you never miss a thing.